Born in Edinburgh in 1906, **John Innes Mackintosh Stewart** was educated at Oriel College, Oxford, where he was presented with the Matthew Arnold Memorial Prize and named a Bishop Frazer's scholar. After graduation he went to Vienna to study Freudian psychoanalysis for a year.

His first book, an edition of Florio's translation of *Montaigne*, got him a lectureship at the University of Leeds. In later years he taught at the universities of Adelaide, Belfast and Oxford.

Under his pseudonym, Michael Innes, he wrote a highly successful series of mystery stories. His most famous character is John Appleby, who inspired a penchant for donnish detective fiction that lasts to this day. His other well-known character is Honeybath, the painter and rather reluctant detective, who first appeared in *The Mysterious Commission*, in 1975.

Stewart's last novel, *Appleby and the Ospreys*, appeared in 1986. He died aged eighty-eight.

D0870903

The Ampersand Papers
Appleby and Honeybath
Appleby and the Ospreys
Appleby At Allington
The Appleby File
Appleby On Ararat
Appleby Plays Chicken
Appleby Talking
Appleby Talks Again
Appleby's Answer
Appleby's End
Appleby's Other Story
An Awkward Lie
The Bloody Wood
Carson's Conspiracy
A Change of Heir
Christmas At Candleshoe
A Connoisseur's Case
The Daffodil Affair
Death At the Chase
Death At the President's Lodging
A Family Affair
From London Far
The Gay Phoenix

Going It Alone
Hamlet, Revenge!
Honeybath's Haven
The Journeying Boy
Lament For a Maker
The Long Farewell
Lord Mullion's Secret
The Man From the Sea
Money From Holme
The Mysterious Commission
The New Sonia Wayward
A Night of Errors
Old Hall, New Hall
The Open House
Operation Pax
A Private View
The Secret Vanguard
Sheiks and Adders
Silence Observed
Stop Press
There Came Both Mist and Snow
The Weight of the Evidence
What Happened at Hazelwood

MICHAEL INNES

HARE SITTING UP

You yourself, don't you find it a beautiful clean thought, a world empty of people, just uninterrupted grass, and a hare sitting up?

D H LAWRENCE, *Women in Love*

This edition published in 2001 by House of Stratus, an imprint of House of Stratus Ltd, Thirsk Industrial Park, York Road, Thirsk, North Yorkshire, YO7 3BX, UK.
Also at: House of Stratus Inc., 2 Neptune Road, Poughkeepsie, NY 12601, USA.

www.houseofstratus.com

Typeset, printed and bound by House of Stratus.

A catalogue record for this book is available from the British Library and the Library of Congress.

ISBN 1-84232-738-0

PART ONE

JUNIPER

1

Juniper had been to Oxford to attend a conference of headmasters of preparatory schools. It was the middle of the long vacation, and he hadn't expected to see many undergraduates. But now, just as his train was about to move out of the station, half a dozen of them tumbled into his compartment. He would have their company non-stop to Paddington. It would be rather a squash.

Actually, there were only five: three men and two girls. As one of the men swung his suitcase up on the rack Juniper noticed that it had been hastily packed. There was the toe of a black sock hanging out at one end, and a scrap of white fur at the other. Of course the scrap of white fur explained matters. It couldn't be anything but a BA hood. These young people were not undergraduates. They were graduates – of perhaps a couple of hours standing. This was a Degree Day, and with hundreds of others who had lately passed their final examinations they had come up for a graduation ceremony. Three young men and two young women. All with their careers before them.

Juniper found himself taking a deep breath. He hadn't much cared for the conference; he wasn't in very good spirits; he was fifty-two. And now here was all this vitality and eagerness crowded round him. Merely as a spectator of it, he had to brace himself by taking this deep breath. Curiously enough, as the train jerked forward, the young man sitting opposite Juniper found it necessary to do precisely the same thing. He took positively a gulp of air.

'Well!' the young man said, ' – goodbye to all that.'

'But it still goes on, remember.' The reply came from a ginger-haired and freckled youth sitting next to Juniper. 'Chaps sweating

3

through their last long vac now. Hungry generations, getting ready to tread us down. Twelve months, Toby my boy, and they'll be after the same jobs that we are.'

Toby stretched out long legs on each side of Juniper's ankles. 'My dear Arthur,' he said comfortably, 'you and I can go a long way in twelve months.'

'And so can the world.' A dark young man sitting in the corner diagonally opposite to Juniper looked up from a book he had opened to offer this. 'Take comfort from that, when you get in a bloody panic job-hunting.' He glanced at the girl sitting next to him. 'Sorry,' he added conventionally.

The girl looked at him in silent scorn. She clearly regarded the habit of apologizing for feeble bad language as beneath contempt. The second girl, who was sitting on the other side of the ginger-haired Arthur, so that Juniper could see nothing of her for the moment except that she was wearing one bright yellow stocking and one bright green, seemed to judge it necessary to bridge an awkward gap. 'Gavin,' she said – apparently meaning the dark young man, 'gets these apocalyptic feelings. There's nothing in them. The great world rolls for ever down the ringing grooves of change. But far more groove than change.'

'*Plus ça change, plus c'est la même chose.*'

The comfortable Toby had produced this. It elicited gasps of ironical admiration all round. Juniper realized that all his travelling companions were acquainted with each other, and they would probably chatter on like this throughout the journey. It might be quite fun. He had nothing to read except a pamphlet which he had picked up at his conference and which he hadn't much expectation of finding absorbing. But he had better keep his nose in it. If he was felt to be an outsider listening, the talkers might become self-conscious and dry up. Arthur had already given him a sharply considering glance. So Juniper managed a frown of concentration over the blur of print in front of him.

And now the girl to whom Gavin had so ineptly apologized spoke crisply. 'But some basic things do change. Things that have remained constant for hundreds of years have changed quite a lot between last year and this year. It's rather striking, really.'

'Do you mean Alice's stockings?' Toby asked. 'They're striking – and quite charming. And I suppose they haven't been happening quite like that since the fifteenth or sixteenth century. Elegant pages in Perugino or Pintoricchio. Terribly nice.'

The girl called Alice, who might have been expected to tuck her legs modestly beneath her at this assault, merely leant forward and scratched her own brightly clothed ankles. 'Jean means nothing of the sort,' she said. 'She means bombs and things.'

'Oh, bombs!' Toby sat back as if withdrawing from the talk. 'Probably I might have said things that have remained constant for millions of years, not just for hundreds.' The brisk Jean was entirely serious. 'Take elks.'

'Elks?' Gavin said. 'Some sort of American freemasons?'

'I mean real elks, particularly in the north of Sweden. The radioactivity in their bones is up by 200 per cent. Contaminated pastures. If Gavin gets apocalyptic feelings, I think he's entitled to them.'

'Isn't it all exaggerated?' Toby asked, as if with a return of mild interest.

'Not so much exaggerated as tricky.' The ginger-haired Arthur was now as serious as Jean. 'Or that's what our Provost tells me. And he's in on radiation, all right. Chief scientific adviser, in fact, to Euratom's health division.'

There was an impressed silence. Juniper let his pamphlet drop into his lap. These young people were now interesting him very much.

'And what does your Provost say?' Alice asked.

'He says that you have to be damned careful what you say. A scare headline in a national paper might persuade thousands of people that it was dangerous to give their babies milk. And public agitation, if it got out of hand, might cripple a government in effective international negotiation.'

'To hell with that, anyway,' Toby said.

Gavin nodded his dark head. 'Yes, to hell with that.'

And Arthur nodded too. 'Well, there I agree with you. I'm all for crippling the bastards if they can be crippled. But can they? Not by protest marches, and being a nuisance to bobbies outside research establishments, and all that stuff.'

'But isn't what you call "all that stuff" the only thing we have to chuck at them?' Jean asked. 'It's like fighting with bottles, I quite agree. But bottles are better than nothing.'

'Certainly they are. But our Provost says another thing about popular agitation. It can do all sorts of mischief just by getting its facts half wrong. Suppose that the strontium rate in grass, or in your elks, Jean, goes bumping up sharply just after the Russians have done a series of experiments. Everybody starts shouting that the experiments have been dirty – dirty in the technical sense, that is. And the Russians say No, not at all, they were frightfully careful to make them as clean as clean. At that we all start shouting – those of us that aren't party-line boys – that Russians are frightful great liars. This might happen, you see, just at a time when there was some chance of a thaw and a general gleam of sense all round. Which would be a disaster. And it would be happening because we hadn't stopped to collect our scientific facts – all our scientific facts. You see, the strontium percentage bumps up and down for other reasons besides bomb tests. Wet weather or dry is quite enough to set the hypersensitive instruments that measure such things swinging one way or the other.'

The well-informed Arthur paused. There was another – and this time rather baffled – silence. Then Jean thought of a relevant question. 'How old is this Provost of yours?' she asked.

'Sixty-nine. He retires next year.'

'Well, that's *him*,' Alice said with decision. 'They just don't, at that sort of age, know what it's all about.'

'Does he,' Toby asked mildly, 'have a stroke every now and then?'

'Or have the surgeons,' Gavin added, 'been obliged to excise the softer bits of his brain?'

'Oh, shut up,' Arthur said crossly. 'We'll all be that age one day.'

'Shall we?' Jean asked. 'I'd say that's rather the point.'

'Well, anyway, they're not decent – personalities like that. Our Provost may have reaction-times like a hearse, but he does ask one to lunch.'

'We can certainly drop him,' Gavin said tolerantly. 'He does no harm in your blessed college, and probably not much on Euratom either. But he's a symptom of something pretty grim, you'll agree. Our fathers, when they were our age, declaimed against government by the grey-haired. But they didn't have to declaim against government by near-corpses. In those days, the really disabling diseases killed fairly quickly. Nowadays, you can have a man sitting at a conference table when there's pretty well nothing left of him except will and judgement. And will can last longer even than judgement in a mortally sick man.'

'That's thoroughly true.'

This time, the silence was a startled one. For it was Juniper who had spoken. He hadn't in the least meant to.

It was the ginger-headed Arthur – he who had already looked curiously at Juniper – who spoke first. He spoke to the accompaniment of a surprisingly sheepish grin, and to an entirely unexpected effect. 'Hullo, sir. I'm afraid we've been failing to recognize each other.'

For a moment Juniper stared at him blankly. Then he laughed. 'Well I'm blessed,' he said. 'It's – '

'Arthur Ferris, '44 to '48.' The ginger-haired youth spoke quickly, in case his former headmaster should in fact be baffled. 'The worst mathematician you ever got into Rugby, sir.'

'I doubt that. Did you overlap with Bingo Parker? Probably not. But the surgeons had certainly been at *his* brain – in his first childhood and not his second – and taken out the bit with sums in it.'

Everybody laughed politely. Since the stranger had joined in their conversation, they felt that this was the thing to do. Probably they were a little sorry for Arthur, who had been gassing away, with this elderly beak of his beside him all the time. It was perhaps because

Juniper was aware of this that he hastened a return to the former general topic.

'I was saying I thought you right about will and judgement. One can never confidently trust the judgement of a very sick man. The will may crack much later.'

'Then isn't it odd, sir,' Toby asked politely, 'that what happens nowadays isn't more disastrous than it is? Really important people seem to be kept alive in the most fantastic way. And their judgement can't be – it can't possibly be – what it was. They dominate contending nations – and yet here we are, alive, and the world at peace, more or less, and nobody's killing anybody else except in quite obscure corners of it.'

Juniper nodded. He guessed that intelligence lurked in the easy-going Toby. 'Perhaps,' he said, 'will is more important than judgement – up at that level. It can't find solutions, but it can block the way. Sit at a table opposite to an absolutely inflexible will and – if you're an absolutely inflexible will yourself – the probable outcome will be just nothing at all. And there's no harm in that. It's budging or being budged that may be fatal.'

The serious Jean sat up straight. Juniper could see at once that she was what they call father-eclipsed. Either she had to crumple before an elderly man or react against him vigorously. 'You mean,' she asked, 'that we should see to it that near-corpses negotiate with near-corpses, and that they need have neither wits in their heads nor compassion in their bowels as long as their jaws set like rat traps?'

Juniper hesitated for a moment. He was aware that the other young people had become slightly uncomfortable. They were all capable of being serious – indeed they liked seriousness – but they hated a hint of any sort of emotional overtone to all this. And before he could frame a reply, the multi-coloured Alice again took on the role of smoothing things over.

'But if you don't budge and he doesn't budge,' she said, 'then you will both go on manufacturing those ghastly things. And bankrupting yourselves in the process. For the expense is astronomical, isn't it?'

'Certainly it is.' Juniper followed this up briskly. 'Killing people gets more and more expensive century by century, and war by war. And when you break down the cost of nuclear fission you get some quite fantastic results. Advertising vacant appointments, for instance. Getting the right man for a moderately senior job often costs £8,000, that way alone.'

Arthur Ferris laughed. 'It would be bad if getting an assistant master cost that, sir.'

'My dear Ferris, I'd regard it as a facer if it cost a thousandth part of it. Even for somebody who can teach mathematics with an eye on Rugby – and I assure you they're much the hardest to get hold of.'

'And it could all be spent on medical research,' Alice said. 'Or on getting millions of people in what Toby calls obscure corners of the world up at least to something near the bread line.'

'They'd only breed faster,' Gavin said.

'That's where medical research would come in.' Alice hesitated for a fraction of a second. 'Contraception's no good as it is – not among primitive peoples. But if you can manage it orally, the old Malthusian nightmare is solved.'

Everybody started talking at once. And Juniper, who knew that his nerves hadn't been too good of late, was suddenly aware that he was almost in a queer way. For, quite out of the blue, he felt affection for these young people – and felt guilty about them too. He liked the small boys at Splaine Croft – he just wouldn't be there if he didn't – but the shades of their prison house were still far off. These young men and women were, so to speak, just ready to be tumbled in. For a still moment, while the chatter ran on, Juniper sat back and wondered what fool or blackguard had made the world into which the tumbling must be done.

It was Toby's voice that brought him back to an awareness of the course of the argument. 'So if people must be killed,' Toby was saying, 'there's everything to be said for doing the job cheaply. It comes to that. Back to Tamburlaine and Genghis Khan.'

'But there's also much to be said for doing it with discrimination,' Juniper said. 'High explosive wasn't too bad there. If you dropped it

MICHAEL INNES

from Zeppelins' – he paused for a moment, wondering if any of his hearers would be very clear about what a Zeppelin was – 'or torpedoed it into a passenger liner, you were at least still more or less taking aim. And even if you blockaded a whole nation, you presumably knew what you were about – if that indeed can be called knowledge, which is, presumably, unaccompanied by imaginative realization.' He paused again, aware that there was a real stillness in the railway compartment. 'But the hydrogen bomb is, of course, quite simply madness. It's spectacularly effective – just as would be some contrivance for ensuring that the earth should fall into the sun. It's indiscriminate to that degree. We bankrupt ourselves, as one of you said, to manufacture something which must destroy us if put into use. So cheap ways of indiscriminate slaughter would be a *little* more rational. And cheap ways of very large-scale but yet *controllable* slaughter would be more rational still. A relative rationality, of course. Considering the whole thing entirely as an inside job.'

There was silence. 'An inside job?' somebody asked.

'Inside the madhouse. My generation are all inside. We're trapped into making all our calculations as if an outside didn't exist. Your generation has the job of breaking out, wouldn't you say?'

'Certainly we have.' Toby stretched his long legs farther on each side of Juniper's shoes. He had the appearance of being very relaxed. 'But we need to get the know-how. A hint or two, say. And I take it you don't mean, sir, that your own generation is entitled simply to abdicate responsibility?'

'Certainly not. But I'm being a bore.' Juniper suddenly felt so tired that he wanted to get out of the whole conversation. 'It's not really stuff for a schoolmaster to pontificate about.'

'You seemed to have some specialized knowledge,' the dark Gavin said abruptly. 'Those £8,000 advertisements, for instance.'

Juniper smiled. 'It's very indirect. A sort of family connexion.'

'We may all have that, in a manner of speaking.' Arthur Ferris spoke after having remained silent for some time. 'I don't know whether you heard us joking about job hunting. Well, we can't tell where any job will land us. Whether we've read Arts or Science, some vast industrial concern is quite likely to suck us in. That's true even of the women – '

'Thank you,' Alice interrupted with spirit. 'Although the probability is that we shall become governesses, no doubt.'

'Don't trail feminist red herrings, Alice dear. I'm saying we're all liable to be sucked into concerns which have what you may call close family relationships with slaughter. There's no escaping it.'

'You can teach,' Juniper said – and knew he said it a little stiffly. 'Not much money. But you can teach in a decent school. I'll get any of you a job tomorrow.'

'But what if we taught sedition?' Toby asked cheerfully. 'Or, if not sedition, at least thoroughly subversive ideas? What if we marched the kids to one of those atom-busting places, and urged them to lie down and bite the bobbies in the calves? It might be keeping schoolmastering going as an honourable profession, if you ask me. But what would the parents say? And what would happen to the fees?'

'What indeed,' Juniper said, and let his tone indicate his disinclination to pursue this line.

'I'm much more interested,' Gavin said at once, 'in something else. It's the twilight of the gods idea – the fascination of bringing everything else down with you as you fall. Hitler was gripped by that, I imagine. But you needn't necessarily be a Wagnerite to feel the tug of it.'

Alice crossed a green leg over a yellow one. 'Death-wish stuff,' she said. 'How does it correlate with actually dying? Does anybody know? You see, we've been talking about the dangers of concentrating power – and far more potential destructive power than has ever existed before – in the hands of old, sick men. Suppose they're dying because they *want* to die – '

'Which is very great rot to begin with,' Toby interrupted cheerfully.

'But I'm just trying to keep an open mind. Would there really be any tendency in an old, sick man – an unconscious tendency, I mean – to take the whole outfit with him?'

For a moment everybody considered this problem soberly. And again Juniper found himself strangely moved – this time, just by the silence. The thought of these young people didn't perhaps go very deep. But they were applying what information they had – including some surprisingly old-fashioned psychological conceptions – to problems that were very real to them. And to him.

'I don't believe in your fatal old men,' Arthur said. 'I'm more ready to be scared of fatal young ones. Chaps just like you and me. The chaps who cruise round with these things in the sky. What about one of them going off his head?'

'But they're not quite like you and me.' Toby said this with ironical conviction. 'They're not highly educatable types like us – and therefore, of course, they're far less neurotic and unstable. Which is fortunate, is it not?'

Once more Jean sat up straight. 'What awful rot! It's been proved again and again that the most surprising people will pack up under strain. And I think Gavin is right with his twilight of the gods stuff. And then, you know – I'm not sure if it's the same thing – there are people obsessed with a violent pathological loathing of the whole human species. I have one in my own family, as a matter of fact. Imagine giving Jonathan Swift a hydrogen bomb.'

'Jonathan Swift?' Arthur asked. 'Is that a chap at Balliol?'

'He wrote a book called *Gulliver's Travels*,' Jean said crushingly. 'As it's a nursery book when the awkward bits have been expurgated, even you might be supposed to have heard of it.'

'All right, all right,' Arthur said, slightly abashed. 'But there *is* a Jonathan Swift at Balliol. I've played squash with him.'

'And have you ever,' Gavin asked, 'played squash with D H Lawrence?'

'A bearded chap at Trinity,' Toby added gravely.

'Of course if you have to talk like idiots – ' Arthur said, gravely offended, and reached for a newspaper.

'Perhaps you'd prefer a book?' Gavin asked, and held out the volume he had opened at the beginning of the journey. 'I'll show you at which end to begin.'

Without rising to this childish insult, Arthur took the book and glanced at the title. '*Women in Love*? I've read that one.'

They had all, it seemed, read *Women in Love* – a fact that surprised Juniper a good deal. But he remembered having been told that, for this generation, Lawrence was the sole novelist to have survived from the beginning of the century.

'Is there something relevant,' he asked Gavin, 'in *Women in Love*?'

'Something frightfully relevant, if you ask me. Do you remember a character called Rupert Birkin? He ends up all cosy and smug with something he calls an ultimate marriage, while his unenlightened friend Gerald Critch walks out into the snow and gets frozen dead like a rabbit. That's the story. But, earlier on, Birkin has this hating mankind in the guts neurosis pretty badly.'

'Lawrence had it himself,' Alice interrupted. And added conscientiously: 'On one side of his complex nature, that is.'

'Birkin,' Gavin continued, 'invites this girl he's going to have his ultimate marriage with to agree that humanity is dry-rotten, and that healthy young men and women are in fact apples of Sodom with insides full of bitter, corrupt ash. Humanity is a huge aggregate lie, and things would be better if every human being perished tomorrow. He asks her – this girl he's going to sleep with, mind you – whether she doesn't find this a beautiful clean thought. No more people. Just uninterrupted grass, and a hare sitting up.'

'A hare sitting up?' Toby asked. 'And nobody with a gun?'

'The beast will degenerate,' Arthur said. 'Nothing to bolt from.'

'And there's a good deal more of it,' Gavin went on. 'Birkin is fanatical. He says he would be ready to die like a shot, to know that the earth would really be swept clean of people. The question is: is there a real mentality like that, or is Lawrence just making it up?' He turned to Juniper, as if in direct challenge. 'What do you think, sir?'

'I think that Birkin is putting in rather a tall order. In point of discrimination, I mean. You remember that we were talking about that? Well, it seems that nowadays getting rid of the human beings wouldn't be too difficult. But I'm not so sure about sparing the hare, or even the grass.'

'Who cares?' Jean asked. 'A lot of *Women in Love* is quite terrific. But Birkin on the hares and the grass is sentimental tosh. I remember Bertrand Russell doing a radio talk about the bomb, and saying something about the innocent birds and trees. Perhaps there are people with whom that sort of thing goes home. But – although, as it happens, I'm rather keen on birds – I'm not one of them. This strikes me as a human world, or nothing.' Jean paused, as if uncertain about her own logic. 'Alice, what do you think?'

'About Birkin in the novel? I remember him as quite harmless. A harmless bore. Nobody who poured out that sort of talk would ever be a danger to anybody. There's a place in the book where some irritated female hits him over the head with a paperweight or something. But all he does in reply is to go out and climb a hill and take his clothes off and roll in the flowers. Ferdinand the Bull couldn't be more innocuous.'

'But if this Birkin,' Toby said, 'believed himself to be an out-and-out do-gooder, full of an exalted love of, and belief in, humanity? If he was a type who is quite noisy in *that* way – but really because he is smothering a still small voice inside himself that is taking the corrupt ash and apples of Sodom line – '

'Over-compensating,' Alice interrupted happily. 'Then, of course, he'd be a frightful danger. Birkin mustn't have the bomb.'

'Birkin didn't *know* about the bomb,' Toby said. 'The interesting – and perhaps daunting – fact is precisely *that*.'

Juniper looked at Toby curiously. He still felt that this long-limbed lounger was, intellectually, the pick of the bunch. 'How do you make that out?' he asked.

'There's something that all the little books, and all the little lectures, tell you about Lawrence. He was a prophet. Wasn't somebody talking about Bertrand Russell? Well, he says that Lawrence had developed the whole philosophy of Fascism before the politicians had thought of it. And with the bomb, you see, it's rather the same. Nobody had dreamed of anything that could wipe out the human race – '

'Martians,' Arthur interrupted. 'There was already lots of science fiction of that sort.'

'Well, yes – but that's a special case, and merely fantastic. My point is that here is Lawrence's Birkin brooding over the image of something which comes within the bounds of sober possibility thirty years later. I don't like it. I'm not sure it doesn't frighten me.'

'Of course,' Alice said, 'it might be a sort of dream-prophecy, all disguised and inside out. It may really be the hares that are wiped out. There was that disease that nearly annihilated the rabbit.'

'And *that*,' Toby said robustly, 'brings up another topic. Bacteriological warfare. Cheaper by a long way, I imagine. But whether it can be used so as not to bounce, I don't know.' He looked across the compartment at Juniper. 'Have you any information on that, sir?'

'None whatever.'

For a moment there was the effect of a full stop. Juniper realized that he must have spoken abruptly.

'I imagine,' Alice said, 'that it's even more hush-hush than bombs. If it really exists.'

'I think it exists,' Juniper said, more mildly. 'In fact, I have a brother who has some information about it. But he never makes it a subject of discussion. No doubt that's because it's as hush-hush as can be.'

'And perhaps,' Jean said, 'because it's about the very nastiest thing that can be thought of? Just as an idea, it seems even nastier than the bomb.'

Juniper nodded. 'I quite agree. At a first glance, the possibility of responsible scientists lending themselves to such investigations seems merely fantastic. And yet one can see how it is. The threat is judged to exist. Means of defence against it must be considered. And so the field, the area of study and experiment, is established.'

'And something else is established too.' Jean's voice shook a little. 'That we really are the most pernicious race of little odious vermin that nature ever suffered to crawl upon the surface of the earth.'

Once more there was the slightly awkward pause that Jean was apt to induce. Alice turned quickly to Arthur. 'Jonathan Swift again,' she said kindly. 'That Balliol man.'

'God be with you, Balliol men,' Gavin quoted solemnly.

They all laughed quickly. Only Juniper – perhaps because he was not young and no longer much subject to the sudden touch of cold fear – alone remained grave.

'Swift on the vermin is all right,' he said. 'But Shakespeare's more succinct.'

'Yes, sir?' Arthur Ferris, as if suddenly reminded of old pupillary days at Splaine Croft, had turned to him expectantly.

'It's a simple statement about self-destruction and the evil in the heart of man:

> *Our natures do pursue,*
> *Like rats that ravin down their proper bane,*
> *A thirsty evil; and when we drink we die.*

I can't remember who is speaking – and it's not important. What the lines carry does seem to me important, and I've often been haunted by them.'

Everybody looked at Juniper curiously – as if after this he must have something more to say. But he remained silent. And presently, as the train ran into Paddington, he did no more than exchange a few words with Ferris as an old Splaine boy. He knew that the talk of these casual travelling companions, unlike the lines from *Measure for Measure*, would soon pass out of his head. He knew that he would probably never again set eyes on Toby, Arthur, and the rest of them. But for a little time, at least, the encounter had disturbed him.

And he knew that it was because he had mentioned his brother – had fingered, in his own mind, an area where a great uneasiness lay.

He took a taxi across to Waterloo – although the tube would have been quite as quick. The taxi provided the feeling, if not the reality, of haste. And he didn't want to look at London, still less to run into any

16

London acquaintance. He just wanted to get quickly to Splaine Croft. It was neurotic, he knew, his recurrent sense of the place as a refuge – precisely as neurotic as the disposition that worried him in his brother. If he really gave the impulse rein, he would be in as desperate a case as those obsessional scholars who scarcely dare venture out of the great womb-like museums and libraries. Whereas Splaine wasn't really a bit like that. It was a place where quite an aggressively creative job was done – both on young bodies and young minds. Even now, in the middle of the holidays, there would be things to tackle as soon as he got back there. If it spelt anything, it spelt sanity. That, for him, was its governing idea – that, or it failed him utterly. So it would be a pity, after just these three days at Oxford, to make his return to that sanity by a route that took him, so to speak, right round the bend.

The trouble, of course, was this family complex, as it must be called. Look how it had been touched off on the train. And needlessly, likely enough. As so often before.

But although he had taken a taxi from Paddington to Waterloo, he walked – comfortably enough, with no more than his outsize briefcase – from Splaine Junction to the school. He liked particularly the short tramp through the village. Tiny though the place was, there might be half a dozen people with whom to pass a confident time of day. He liked the smell of the smithy – a smell that still came straight out of childhood. He liked, in the window of the dairy, the enormous and highly polished milk can that never ceased to enchant the boys when they came down to spend their pocket money. It had an elaborately engraved inscription: *Special Cows kept for Invalids and Infants.* There was a tradition of daring new boys to go in and ask if they might see the special cows. Juniper supposed that once the special cows must really have existed – for commercial ballyhoo had been only in its infancy when that legend had been engraved on the shining metal. But what had been special about them? There was a real subject for research in that.

Juniper turned through the lodge gates and gave a wave to Currill, the groundsman, who was putting in a little work in his own neat garden. The roof of the school – a pleasant tumble of quite spurious Tudor gables – appeared for a moment through a gap in the trees. Then it vanished until Juniper came round the last sweep of the drive. He heard boys' voices from one of the broad tiled verandas. Yes, there they were, the little holiday crowd: three regulars whose parents were in Africa or the Far East – distinguishable by their regulation blue corduroy shorts and windcheaters – and along with them eight or nine holiday visitors, recruited to help with the overheads. But recruited, too, to keep the place alive other than at the purely economic level. Splaine Croft was a dismal place without boys: a slightly vulgar Edwardian country house degraded into a derelict barracks. But when the boys were there, you didn't notice how the once handsome appointments had been kicked to bits – or you didn't notice, provided you had a taste for boys mucking around. In term-time there were seventy-eight of them. And almost all the time, they seemed to be tumbling about in form-rooms or corridors or the stable-yard or the playing fields. There couldn't be less regimentation anywhere in England. It was surprising that they did rather well.

The boys playing on the veranda looked up only for a moment as Juniper climbed the steps to the front door. They knew that the headmaster, although a noticing sort of person, hadn't much fancy for being noticed; he preserved with his pupils, precisely as he did with his staff, the sort of courteous aloofness into which some men grow with middle age. So, entirely unselfconsciously, the boys went on with their game. They were playing marbles.

No doubt – Juniper thought as he opened the door and stepped into the familiar cavernous hall – there were prep schools at which marbles would be terribly infra dig. But not here. Every year they had their regular two weeks craze before being succeeded by something else. What usually came after marbles was lead bombs.

Yes – bombs. Juniper frowned as he remembered his railway journey. But at Splaine Croft a bomb meant a species of plummet at the end of a string, cut horizontally in two to permit the insertion of the sort of cap commonly fired in a toy pistol. You let the bomb drop sharply on a hard surface, and a satisfactory explosion was the result.

Splaine boys had never heard real bombs drop. They were too young. But that didn't hold of boys of public-school age, and still less of his late travelling companions. Among people of that generation one must occasionally meet, without being aware of it, young men and women who, as small children, had seen parents or brothers or sisters –

Juniper didn't continue the thought. There were matters in his own experience that must excuse his turning ostrich from time to time. I am a schoolmaster now, he told himself, with a defined and compassable constructive job. Of course, it's a job among the savages – for what are small boys if not that? And savages like a big bang, or at least a middle-sized one in a lead plummet. Or do they? Isn't it a compulsion, rather than a liking? In Oxford, only the day before, he had made the acquaintance of a master from a large midland grammar-school. And this man had told him that almost the only thing the common run of older boys now read is war books. Fictionalized accounts of war in the jungle, of savage guerilla fighting, of men driven to starvation and the verge of madness in prison camps: these easily headed the list. Pleasure was an ambiguous word, surely, to apply to what they got from such stuff. It looked as if the little boys with their bombs and the big boys with their paperbacks were alike trying to get rid, in fantasy, of kinds of fear, of horror, lodged – well, say lodged obstinately by this time in the consciousness of the race…

A schoolmaster, he repeated to himself. That's me. Plain Miles Juniper, responsible for these boys, and doing what I can. Perhaps one can tutor it out of them: the fear and what plants it there – the darkness in the heart of man. It's not a very good bet. But try it.

A bell clanged harshly above the stables.

The bell clanged as usual. In term-time the racket made by the seventy-eight boys would have increased for a moment as if challenged by it – and then there would have been a quick diminuendo as the assistant masters emerged from common room and took charge. But now it was merely calling the holiday bunch to tea. And there were no masters left at the school; only a couple of undergraduates doing a holiday job in order – Juniper suspected – to buy themselves unnecessary luxuries, or to be able to go off to Switzerland and break their legs at Christmas. But they were nice enough lads, and they had plenty of time for reading, supposing them to be inclined that way. A small domestic staff – skeletal, invisible, and entirely competent – ran the place. Apart from that, there was only the school secretary, old Miss Grimstone. And here she was – arthritic and myopic but formidable – emerging from her den-like office.

'A visitor,' Miss Grimstone said. 'Mr Clwyd.'

Juniper looked rather warily at the secretary. There was always a ring of challenge in her ancient voice.

'Mr what?' he asked.

'C-L-W-Y-D. He was most anxious to spell it out. I suppose he's a prospective parent.'

'We don't often get Welsh boys at Splaine.'

Miss Grimstone shook her head. 'Well, at least he's not discernibly Welsh. And I only suppose that he's a parent. He seems a little old for it. A grandfather, perhaps, and thinking of making advance payments by covenant.' Miss Grimstone gave a low chuckle. She was one eminently well-informed on the financial aspect of private education.

'Tax fiddle of some kind? I don't like that sort. But I suppose we can't send him away.'

'Certainly we can't.' Miss Grimstone was indignant. 'Those arrangements are perfectly legal and proper. Nobody is obliged to regulate his monetary affairs so as positively to attract taxation. And if people have to educate each other's children in order *not* to attract it, that is the mere folly of government. And Mr Clwyd is most distinguished. He has a small white beard.'

'Bother his beard. It's probably a fake, like his expense account. And he's just waiting? I certainly made no appointment with him.'

'People do sometimes remember hearing of the school when motoring past, and call in. That's how we got Lord Scattergood's boy.'

'Bother Lord Scattergood's boy. This Clwyd has come by car?'

'A Rolls, Mr Juniper. And with a chauffeur. The man has taken it round to the kitchens and is being given tea. Mr Clwyd himself declined.'

'Well, I suppose I must show him round, and so forth. Has he been waiting long?'

'Less than twenty minutes. I rang through to the station and made sure you had come off the train. And now I must be getting back to next term's bills.'

Miss Grimstone turned away and hobbled into her office. Juniper paused for a moment to collect himself. Splaine Croft was far from crying out for pupils. So he didn't feel at all like a spider luring the bearded Clwyd into his parlour. This fact made him all the more civil to his visitor when he walked into the study and encountered him. 'Mr Clwyd?' he said politely.

Mr Clwyd, who had been reading *The Times*, rose and bowed. 'Mr Juniper?'

'Yes. And I'm so sorry I wasn't in when you called. Do you smoke?' And Juniper pushed forward a cigarette box.

'Thank you, no.' Mr Clwyd was a person of gravity. He possessed a searching but inoffensive gaze which he directed upon Juniper with unabashed frankness. 'I apologize for coming in out of the blue.'

'Not at all.' Juniper, feeling it fair to answer scrutiny with scrutiny, took a good straight look at Clwyd. The beard was a beautifully trimmed affair. At the same time it was in some obscure way ever so faintly unexpected. Apart from this, Juniper's impression was entirely favourable. He felt he knew at once what sort of parent or grandparent Clwyd would be. He wouldn't be a pest, but he would expect a good deal. Nor would he waste time in seeing that he got it. He might be – at a guess – chairman of one of the joint stock banks. He had a timetable for today and every other day, and he had the art of conducting in apparent leisure interviews which he knew would in fact end in twelve or in twenty-five minutes' time. Juniper decided to cut out any remarks about the weather.

'How can I help you?' he asked. It was the association with banking that prompted him to this form of words. His own bank manager said just that.

'You can show me your cricket field.'

'Why – certainly.' Juniper rose, greatly surprised. He knew that there were prospective parents capable of beginning their investigations decidedly on the athletic side, but it hadn't struck him that Mr Clwyd – who so clearly belonged if not to the intellectual at least to the managerial classes – might be one of them. 'We can go out by this window. There's a sett of badgers in the corner over by Splaine Wood, if you're interested in that sort of thing. And as for the pitch – well, it's not too bad. I've got a very reasonable groundsman now, I'm glad to say.'

With this and other professional patter, Juniper led the way into the open air. Mr Clwyd was seriously attentive – but less, Juniper felt, to the substance of the information he was receiving than to the manner in which it was being offered to him. Clwyd walked with deliberation; he carried an umbrella and gloves; he wore a bowler hat not very well accommodated to a summer afternoon in the country. But, despite all this, there was again the impression that he was very little disposed to waste time. He might almost have been in a hurry – and in a hurry to size Juniper up. Juniper didn't reflect that his awareness of this in his visitor was the consequence of a not wholly common acuteness of perception in himself. And although there was something in the situation that made him indefinably uneasy, he nevertheless continued with what he privately called sales talk – and still on the assumption that Mr Clwyd was chiefly, or even exclusively, interested in games. They had beaten their chief rivals, Merton House, handsomely this year. And next year it looked as if they were going to have a really promising slow bowler.

Mr Clwyd gave these remarks his attention until they reached the actual pitch. He even prodded the pitch in a considering way with his umbrella. Then he spoke again for the first time since they had left the study.

'Mr Juniper, my name isn't Clwyd. Nor is this my beard. I'm not sure you haven't guessed as much.'

Juniper was sufficiently perturbed to come abruptly to a halt. And at this the man who was not Mr Clwyd came to a halt too, raised his umbrella and pointed it towards the nearer horizon. He might have been engaged in some polite topographical inquiry.

'I'm afraid I don't understand you, sir.' Juniper spoke with a proper stiffness. He was quite sure that his visitor wasn't mad, and he saw no occasion for tenderness. 'Are we not wasting each other's time?'

'I propose to waste as little time as possible. Mr Juniper, I have asked you to bring me out to your cricket field because it is a spot where we quite certainly can't be overheard.' The visitor paused, made a half turn, and this time pointed with the same air of courteous interest to a nearby spinney. 'It's most unlikely that we are being watched, but you will have to forgive this professional pantomime, all the same.'

'Do I understand that you are an actor, sir?' It was in as chilly a tone as he could manage that Juniper asked this question. He was beginning to feel angry – angry and, he had to admit to himself, alarmed. It was the same alarm – to be more frank, it was the same acute private anxiety – that had welled up into consciousness during his railway journey.

'No, not an actor.' The man who had called himself Clwyd was looking at Juniper steadily. 'I am a policeman,' he said. 'My name is Appleby.'

PART TWO

APPLEBY

1

Standing by the worn crease, with the ferrule of his incongruously urban umbrella thrusting inquisitively at the cavity left by a leg stump, Appleby continued to eye his host with a steady glance. Would *this* Juniper, he was wondering, have what it would take? The question was decidedly that.

'Appleby? Sir *John* Appleby?' the pitch of Juniper's voice had shot up queerly. He was plainly startled.

'Yes. It's odd that you should have heard of me.'

'Surely no odder than this pantomime, as you call it. May I ask why you have presented yourself in this fashion at Splaine Croft?'

So far, so good, Appleby thought. He's a strung-up type, and already he has something on his mind. But he doesn't take things lying down. If he thought me a little younger than I am, he'd be quite ready to turn me out. Except that he guesses something, really. I think he guesses.

Aloud, he said: 'In this fashion? It's a fair question, certainly. The answer, Mr Juniper, is that it absolutely mustn't be suspected that either Scotland Yard or any of the security services has contacted you. As for why I'm here at all – well, I'm afraid that involves rather bad news. Or worrying news, anyway.'

'Is it about my – ?' Juniper checked himself, and appeared to articulate with difficulty. 'Is it about my brother?'

'I am sorry to say it is. Your brother has vanished.'

For a moment it seemed to Appleby that Juniper was completely at sea – as if he had suddenly been addressed in a language unknown to him. 'Disappeared?' When at length he spoke his voice was oddly mechanical. 'Howard *disappeared*? It's not possible.'

'It is possible, and it has happened.' Appleby was now uncompromisingly brisk. 'No doubt the news is a shock, but you have to face it. Professor Juniper walked out of his laboratory at noon on Wednesday. That's three days ago. And he hasn't been seen since.'

'But surely it's not – not necessarily sinister? Mayn't there be some mistake? Howard's gone to a conference, and failed to leave word. Something like that. There are a hundred possible explanations.'

'Mr Juniper, why has this news been such a shock to you?'

Juniper had started unconsciously to walk down the length of the cricket pitch, and Appleby was keeping up with him. But now he halted, and the two men faced each other.

'A shock to me? Well, of course – if it's true.'

'Isn't there something more to it than that? Doesn't this come, Mr Juniper, as – well, something you've feared for a long time?'

'That Howard might' – Juniper hesitated – 'might cut and run? And in a way that sets the head of Scotland Yard on his heels? For that's what you are, aren't you?'

'Something of the sort, Mr Juniper. And, if you want to know the size of the thing, I may say that I am dealing with the matter on the direct instructions of the Prime Minister. Your brother is decidedly among the people who mustn't disappear – not for twelve hours, let alone seventy-two. To put it quite simply, there's a headline we just can't afford to see in the newspapers.'

'A headline?' Juniper seemed merely bewildered again.

'*Top Secret Scientist Missing*. Something like that.'

'Of course, I know that Howard's at the top. And I know what his work is. It was all – it was all in my head this afternoon.'

'This afternoon?' Appleby spoke sharply.

'No, no – it's nothing relevant. Just because of what some young people were discussing.' With a great effort, Juniper seemed to pull himself together. 'Why do you think I have been anxious about Howard? Am I supposed to have been suspecting that he might bolt to Russia? Or merely that he might go mad?'

'Merely that he might go mad.'

Juniper took a deep breath. 'You're frank,' he said. 'I'll try to be too.'

'Thank you. And madness – real madness – need have nothing to do with it. Indeed, it's rather unlikely. But serious nervous breakdown is another matter. Professor Juniper probably works under considerable pressure – '

'Considerable pressure be damned!' Juniper's promise of frankness realized itself abruptly in sudden and surprising passion. 'You know what Howard has been drawn into, as well as I do. If he has gone mad, I don't blame him. Perhaps it's the best thing he can do. And I say be damned to you all. Be damned to your Prime Minister and his Cabinet, and be damned to their opposite numbers in every corner of the globe. And be damned to you and me for suffering them. The guilt's immeasurable. *My* guilt's immeasurable.'

'You're not your brother's keeper.'

But Juniper took a deep breath. It was, Appleby thought, as if something that had been bottled up in this quiet schoolmaster was bursting out in sustained vehemence. 'Yes, I am. At that level we're all each other's keeper. And we're all what the journalists call guilty men. Howard is an honest scientist. He has the misfortune to be also a very good one – in his own line, the best of his age. And devoted, dedicated. Perhaps only I know the sheer toil that has gone to his achievement. And what happens? He is persuaded, on his conscience, to apply himself to devising defence against bacteriological warfare. What does that mean? It means – it means what I was telling some young people only this morning. It means straight out thinking on the means of waging that warfare. Isn't that so?'

'It is undoubtedly so – God help us all.' Appleby gave his answer soberly. 'Perhaps those aren't the official terms. But the fact is just that. Preparation for defence, and preparation for attack: one can't pass the finest blade between them. And if the thing has driven your brother mad, I'm with you in every damn. The question is, though, just what, as practical men, can we do about the existing situation? May we go on to consider that?'

There was a pause. Appleby had been studying his man as he spoke. And his conclusions encouraged him. This Juniper, too, looked as if he had devotion and dedication in him. He wasn't, perhaps, a strong man. But he would put up a stiff fight against his own weakness. And that, it seemed to Appleby, was pretty well the definition of courage. He decided to plunge with Miles Juniper.

'But what is the existing situation?' Juniper was entirely controlled again. 'You say that Howard has vanished, and you suggest it may be a matter of a serious nervous breakdown. I've heard of that sort of thing happening – with or without complete loss of memory going along with it. There's some technical term for it.'

'Fugue, I think. It may be simply hysterical. In that case it usually doesn't last long; the chap may get back on an even keel without treatment, and it may never happen again. On the other hand, it may be a symptom of something more serious blowing up. It's clear that previous history is important. So, if your brother doesn't turn up at once, we shall want you to tell all you know about him – about his health and personality and so on – to the experts.'

Juniper nodded. 'I can see that – of course. And I'll do all I can. I only wish you'd brought those experts along.'

'I rather have it in mind to get you to them.'

'Good. I'm ready. There's not much doing here at the moment. And of course I'd come at once even if there was.' Juniper paused. 'But it's still only one hypothesis, isn't it?'

'This of sudden nervous illness? Certainly it is.' Appleby was now striding across the cricket field, with Juniper keeping pace with him. 'There are other possibilities we have to think of. Serious accident, for instance, in some exceptional circumstances that delay identification. And it's true that, with a man like your brother, my people in London think in terms of the ports and airfields at once. You won't judge me offensive if I say that we have already been hard at work on any background that might suggest *that* sort of cut and run. And I see no evidence whatever that – '

'That Howard has nipped off with his bugs to Moscow?' Juniper spoke without resentment; it was clear that he was merely amused.

'Or, better perhaps, to some nasty small country that can't afford anything more spectacular? No, Sir John' – Juniper was serious again – 'there's nothing in that particular nightmare, as far as Howard's concerned. We can cut it out. So would you mind telling me more of the facts – and what you propose?'

Appleby raised his umbrella and pointed. 'May I propose that we walk over and have a look at that swimming pool? I take no chances in an affair like this. Even to your secretary, please, I remain just another inquiring parent.'

They walked across the August grass, faintly brown. From the edge of the field a breeze, still warm, brought the scent of grass-mowings now rotting. It was familiar and precious, and for a moment Appleby had an odd sense that he was really doing what he was pretending to do: looking over a school to which he was thinking of sending a son. He had indeed done it often enough – but his own children were beyond private school age now. 'I like everything here,' he said suddenly. 'And I wish I wasn't bringing you this bad news – that I wasn't merely pretending to be a parent.'

Juniper looked at him rather oddly. 'Thank you,' he said. 'My secretary took you for a grandparent, actually. But' – he spoke with a touch of mockery – 'no doubt that's the beard.'

Appleby smiled. 'I do apologize for it again. And I'd repeat that it's a fantastic degree of caution. There are people – as I'll explain to you – who would be very interested indeed in the notion of a Professor Howard Juniper vanished into the blue, and of Scotland Yard hurrying down to see his brother. But, to the best of my knowledge, the disappearance is a secret still. I'll explain that too. It will bring me to my real proposal.'

'I'm waiting for that,' Juniper said.

The pool was drained and empty. But the garden boy who was cleaning out the mud and leaves had gone away, and they were again quite alone. Only from the school there came a sudden faint confusion of voices. The holiday crowd had emerged from tea. Perhaps they had discovered the prosperous Mr Clwyd's Rolls Royce.

Appleby paced out the length of the pool. He might have been a veritable Mr Clwyd, checking up with mercantile caution upon the dimensions as declared in the school prospectus. 'You know,' he said, 'how your brother lives: an unmarried man like yourself – and like yourself, right on the job. But – I gather – as something of a recluse. Certainly rather an aloof figure, as far as the staff at the research station goes.'

Juniper nodded. 'Quite so. And I understand it very well. Howard and I are worlds apart in intellectual endowment. That hardly needs saying. But in temperament I imagine that we are notably akin. And that sort of shyness, or whatever it is, grows on both of us with age.'

Again Appleby smiled. 'I think I'd have guessed as much. And, at the moment, there's one important consequence. With the exception of Dr Clandon, his principal assistant, there's as yet nobody to know that the professor's absence isn't perfectly regular. Clandon covered up at once with the small domestic staff; and the scientific people have precisely the notion you had: that your brother's at a conference, or something of the sort. So there we are. At the moment, no sensation. And no alerting of the relevant espionage people.'

Juniper drew a long breath, 'Surely not *that*? It sounds like a shocker. There can't really be – foreign agents who would be interested in the idea of my brother wandering about ill?'

Appleby shook his head rather grimly. 'Shocker or not, there certainly are. And I'm taking no risks. I'm going to find your brother before they do. With luck, I'm going to find him before anybody knows he has to be found. If you will help, that is to say.'

'I've already said I'll help in any way I can.' Juniper was suddenly impatient. 'Good God, man – does it need saying? Howard and I have gone our different ways, and no longer see a great deal of each other. But we're closer to one another than perhaps most brothers are.'

'So far, so good. You see, although Clandon is doing his best, we can't cover up for much longer.'

'But is that really the right thing, Sir John – really necessary? Surely if Howard is missing – and perhaps, as you suggest, a very sick man – it's in his interest and that of everybody else that there should be an alarm and an extensive search?' Juniper seemed now perplexed, anxious, and on the verge of renewed anger.

'There's an extensive search, all right.' Appleby strolled across the grass verge of the swimming pool and glanced into the gloomy changing shed, so that it was almost as if he suspected Professor Howard Juniper of being in hiding there. 'But – I can't too emphatically repeat – I'd rather know where he is before it becomes known that he isn't where he ought to be.'

'Very well. You are the judge. But I record that I consider it thoroughly dangerous.'

'You protest?'

'I don't protest. I simply put that on the record.' For a moment Juniper seemed entirely the rather pedantic schoolmaster. 'Now, go ahead.'

But Appleby, for some reason, paused to take a wider view of the scene. He raised his umbrella and pointed at a beech wood beyond the little river from which Splaine Croft took its name. He might have been talking timber. Then he turned and looked at the school. 'I think I heard some boys?' he asked. 'You have holiday boarders?'

'Only a handful.' Juniper was impatient.

'So the school is fairly empty?'

'There's certainly oceans of room.' Juniper glanced at Appleby and gave a sudden exclamation. 'Great heavens! You don't imagine that – that I'm *hiding* my brother – sheltering him?'

Appleby smiled faintly. 'You are, if I may say so, Mr Juniper, most promisingly acute. And I try to imagine everything under the sun. It's my job.'

'Very well. You can bring down the whole flying squad – if that's what it's called – and search the place. But, meanwhile, and while you're pursuing some damned fantasy, Howard may be in real and sober danger.'

'It's not a point I'm likely to overlook. And we're not, I hope, going to quarrel. Let me come at once to what I want you to do. I want you – just for a vital few days – to take your brother's place.'

Juniper stared at his visitor, thunderstruck. 'Take Howard's place! I'm to be involved in pantomime too! It's impossible. And there's no sense in it. You can't be serious.'

'I'm perfectly serious, and you know it. And it can't be impossible, since you've done it before.'

'Done it before?' Juniper now looked bewildered. 'Just how much have you ferreted out about Howard and me?'

'I know that you are identical twins, and amazingly like each other. I know that when you were both up at Cambridge you played some famous tricks on the strength of it. And I know that it went along with a certain amount of regular theatrical activity – the Footlights, and so forth. Do you happen to have kept up your amateur acting?'

'No, I haven't – although Howard has, to a certain extent. He is altogether more versatile than I am.'

Appleby was carefully testing the flexibility of the diving board. 'I wonder,' he said, 'whether that tells us anything about the probabilities or possibilities of your brother's situation now?'

'Yet more false beards, and so forth, Sir John?' Juniper seemed to intend to speak ironically, but to be veering towards anger again instead. 'It's certainly conceivable that Howard is play-acting. He may have disguised himself as a commercial traveller in order to seduce the wife of a greengrocer. Or a dozen other things – provided you're willing to ignore plain common sense. If Howard is himself, he may be doing something slightly freakish, but not anything downright irresponsible. I'm certain of that. If he's had this nervous breakdown, it's at least my guess that any sort of deliberate disguising of himself is most unlikely. I mean, simply in the light of what sick men do and don't do. But I'm not an expert. I may be wrong there.'

Appleby nodded thoughtfully. 'I imagine you have clinical experience on your side. But there's an exception to every rule. And Professor Juniper, of course, must be an exceptional man to start with. Are you often anxious about him?'

The sudden question took Juniper by surprise, as it was meant to do. But his answer seemed to come frankly enough. 'Well, yes – I am. Ever since he has been on this secret work. We've already touched on that, haven't we? The moral burden must be almost unbearably onerous. If I had to carry it, I think it would make me completely unscrupulous.'

'Unscrupulous?' Appleby took up the word curiously. 'A strong sense of moral responsibility would make you unscrupulous?'

Juniper was frowning, rather as if his perception was still obscure to him. 'Yes – in a sense. I'd feel that I lived in a world of moral imbeciles, against whom I must defend myself by any means in my power – including, perhaps, just clearing out. Something like that.'

'You have a strong sense of sympathy with your brother?'

'Haven't I made that clear?' Juniper turned away impatiently.

'Then you will come to the rescue in the way I've suggested?'

'Yes, I will. If you can show me it isn't nonsense, that is to say.'

'Very well.' Appleby turned away from the swimming pool and began to walk in the direction of the school. He seemed to be confident that the interview would now soon be over. 'What I have to show you is that, if he is known to be wandering round in some more or less helpless state, your brother's danger is acute. I can do that – although you may feel that what I have to tell you about foreign agents, and so forth, is like stuff out of a book. But there's more of – well, more of the same order. Professor Juniper has vanished. That's strange enough. But there's something that takes a good deal more swallowing – and that makes the dangerousness of the situation extend far beyond your brother himself.'

Juniper stopped in his tracks, and Appleby saw that he had quite suddenly gone deadly pale. 'You can't mean – '

'Yes. You yourself came quite near to mentioning it, if only as a sort of joke. Your brother may have taken something with him. Something that ought never to have left a locked refrigerator in his laboratory.'

'It can't be true!' Juniper's voice had risen in pitch again. 'Howard would never – Why, it's madness!'

Appleby turned and looked at him steadily. 'Isn't madness,' he asked, 'one of the possibilities we've been talking about?'

The summer sun, low in a clear sky, was at play on the rambling red-tiled roof of Splaine Croft. It made the place blaze like fire. From the paddock on the other side of the house came the shouts of boys playing tip and run. Appleby, his bowler hat on his head, walked towards the building as if his next task was to check up on its sanitation.

For some moments Juniper walked silently beside him. When he spoke, it was still incoherently. The man – Appleby saw – was really shaken.

'I won't believe it! You said something out of a book. It's that – but absurd, banal. The demented scientist with the vital secret in his pocket? I just won't take it. I doubt the whole thing…your whole visit…who are you… It's a hoax – a hoax in filthy taste.'

Appleby allowed a minute for this disturbance to subside. 'No,' he said presently. 'This is quite literally no joke, Mr Juniper. You know that, really. But I admit that it is all close neighbour to absurdity. The atom bomb in the attaché case. They made rather a good film out of that, although not perhaps a very plausible one. The bomb was certainly a bit much. And of course – inside the story, I mean – it could have been checked up on at once. One can go in and count such things, I suppose, on their racks. Bombs don't obligingly breed for you.'

There was a silence during which Juniper was clearly striving for self-control. 'That assistant,' he brought out presently. 'Clandon, did you call him? Is he certain?'

'No. He can't be certain. The whole technical set-up, it seems, is such that he can't be certain. Your brother is the only person who can be certain.'

'I accept it. I accept your story…the situation.' Juniper, although he spoke firmly, was like a man slightly dazed. 'And I'll go – I'll go at once, and hold the fort as best I can. Although I never expected to be the cuckoo, so to speak, in my brother's scientific nest.'

Appleby smiled grimly. 'It's not a very exact image. But I'm glad you're game. Thank you.'

'I'll need a lot of briefing. But I suppose I can get it from this fellow Clandon. He's to be in the secret, I suppose?'

'He must be. But he's entirely reliable. I know him quite well. A man of some imagination, as well as a competent scientist. He's absolutely willing to see you through as Professor Howard Juniper for a few days.'

'You know…it's funny.' Juniper had come to a halt and was gazing with unseeing eyes at Splaine Croft. 'Did I tell you how I travelled from Oxford today with a lot of young people? I was led into talking to them about all this sort of thing. The whole nightmare, I mean, of these new ways of making war – if war is not far too clean a name for the horror. I think I even mentioned having a brother who was a little concerned in it. The thing slipped out – although not, I hope, indiscreetly. It shows that my anxieties about Howard have been very near the surface of my mind. But I never dreamed of this – that my brother may be carrying round death and destruction with him.'

'I'm sure you didn't.' Appleby, who appeared to be a born actor, meditatively stroked his false beard. 'It would be a distinctly morbid mind that would think up anything of the sort clean out of the blue.'

'But it's true?' Juniper appealed oddly for confirmation, as if he had a lingering hope that he had got the whole thing wrong. 'Howard may actually have taken – have taken something almost as destructive as an atom bomb?'

'*Almost as destructive!*' Appleby paused, apparently thinking better of going on. 'Clandon will be the man to tell you about that.'

Juniper was very pale again. 'All right,' he said. 'I think my own imagination can cope with the possible dimensions of the thing. Now, how had I better get away? I'm ready this instant.'

Appleby nodded approvingly. 'Mr Clwyd,' he said, 'will take a quick look at a form room and a dormitory, and drive off. You'll get a telegram within half an hour. It will be a genuine telegram from – shall we say Dorchester? But it will have begun its life on the short-wave transmitter in my car. Would the sudden death of an old friend serve?'

'Quite adequately, I suppose. And he can be given any name under the sun. Even Miss Grimstone – that's my secretary – hasn't a line on my whole former acquaintance.'

'Very good. You will pack your bag, and mention to the relevant people that you are an executor of your late friend's estate, and that after the funeral you may be detained by business for some days.'

Juniper frowned. 'I suppose,' he asked, 'there must be a funeral?'

And Appleby caught his meaning. '*Absit omen*,' he said.

2

Three days later Dr Herbert Clandon came to see Appleby. He was a large comfortable rumbling man, but his comfortableness didn't prevent his being at present heavy-eyed and anxious.

'No news?' he said, when he had shaken hands.

'Not a glimmer.' Appleby was far from looking carefree himself.

'Nice view you have here.' Clandon, who wasn't the sort of person that one bothered to ask to sit down, had strolled over to the window and was looking over the Thames. 'Top man gets choice of room – eh?'

'Just that.'

'Never happen to me.' Clandon rumbled contentedly. He was aristocratic, wealthy, and an FRS 'Back room boy'. He accepted a cigarette from the box held out to him. 'Not a glimmer, you say? Now, that would be significant of what?'

'Certainly not of Professor Juniper's wandering around, harmlessly mad. We'd have picked him up by now. If that was the initial situation, it's over.'

Clandon nodded. 'So I'd have supposed, Appleby. Let's face it.'

'Let's face it, by all means. Of course, it mayn't have been the initial situation at all. He may have walked out, as sane as you are, to a prepared hide-out where he can be snug till the Greek Kalends.'

'Or till Kingdom Come – which is better English, my boy.' Clandon had enjoyed a nodding acquaintance with Appleby for a long time.

'Alternatively, he may have had an equally well-prepared plan to leave the country. No highly intelligent man would find difficulty in evolving one.'

'Clearly not. Nor is it difficult to drown oneself with a millstone round one's neck – if one's intent on leaving behind one as much mystery and anxiety as possible.' Clandon rumbled again – but gloomily this time. 'I don't think, by the way, that you've mentioned what must be the commonest occasion of a fellow's cutting the painter.'

'Something about a woman?' Appleby shook his head. 'My sense of the matter is all against that, somehow.'

'And I think you're right. Howard never had any interest in women, as far as I could see. Or in sex in general. Which doesn't mean, mark you, that he was extravagantly out of the way. Plenty of busy men just never bother. They don't, somehow, get into novels and plays and suchlike trash. But they exist. This brother's rather the same, I'd say.' Clandon came lumbering over to Appleby's desk. He was dressed in tweeds so hairy as to suggest some sort of cave man. 'You've landed me, by the way, with the hell of an assignment there.' Clandon rumbled more than ever. 'I admit it has been a good idea. But it's a headache, I don't mind telling you. Bloody bad actor, Howard's brother the usher. Even now that he's calmed down a bit.'

'Bad, is he?' Appleby was rather surprised. 'Tell me all about it. You don't think anybody has guessed?'

'Lord, no. Our crowd has no eyes for anything outside a test-tube, thank goodness. Getting the deception going was perfectly easy. As soon as brother Miles arrived I whisked him into Howard's private lab, dressed him up in a white coat, and had in a couple of junior people just to get a word from myself. So it went round at once that the Head Man was back. Lucky that brother Miles didn't have to put up more of a show at the start. He was in a poor way.'

'He was sufficiently strung up when I saw him at his school and gave him the news. But I'm rather surprised by what you say. Miles struck me as quite tough, down below. And the brothers used to play ball with each other's identities long ago. So the job oughtn't to have been too disconcerting. Although it's Howard, it seems, who has been a bit of an actor since.'

'Certainly it isn't the usher, as I'll make clear. But first – about his being in a state. That hasn't lasted, thank goodness. The next morning, he was a different man.'

'A different man?' In its particular context, Appleby found this phrase startling.

Clandon roared with laughter. 'One can see it turning into an old-fashioned farce,' he said. 'First twin going out by the door and second twin climbing in by the window. But all I mean is that this Miles had got a grip on himself. He was far less anxious.'

'About his ability to carry the impersonation through?'

Clandon looked doubtful. 'Well, I suppose so. Although if he thought he was being good at it, he was quite confoundedly wide of the mark. Still, there it was. If you'd been able to weigh his quantum of anxiety on a balance, I'm pretty sure you'd have found that about half of it had evaporated.'

Appleby considered this. 'Perhaps it was a sudden swing to over-confidence?'

'Perhaps it was. Part of the trouble with his passing himself off as Howard during these last two days has been that there's been no discretion about it. He's drifted round the labs – and even entered into conversation with people – far more than has been necessary. And it isn't, as I've said, as if he were capable of putting up a virtuoso performance. I've seen him make several hair-raising blunders myself.'

'How very odd.' Appleby had risen from his desk and himself paced rather restlessly to a window. 'Rusty, in a manner of speaking – wouldn't that be it? Nothing like up to his old level of performance, and yet instinctively aiming at it.'

'It's an idea.' Clandon sounded dubious.

'Consider the sort of turns the two brothers used to put on as lads. You must have heard of some of them.'

'I've heard' – Clandon rumbled with renewed cheerfulness – 'that Howard played Rugger for England. Eighty thousand people looking on, and supposing that it was Miles scoring the vital try against Ireland.'

41

'Precisely.' Appleby swung round to face the room. 'To you and me, a thing like that is amusing and admirable. But think of the scandal, if it had ever come out officially: a rowing Blue – which is what Howard was – smuggling himself into an International Rugger match! Think of all the old gentlemen who played against Wales in '97, and so on. Criminal irresponsibility would be their verdict. Fellow who could do that, sir, ought to be ducked in a horse-pond. Wouldn't that be the reaction?'

Clandon nodded. 'Certainly it would. No doubt as undergraduates the terrible Juniper twins made their fun as risky and outrageous as possible. But would that really prompt Miles to be unnecessarily venturesome – now, in this desperately serious situation? No, I think it must be simply that he lacks judgement. And technique. He's simply just not a convincing Professor Howard Juniper. But, I dare say, we can get by for a few days more. At least the man isn't the nervous wreck he showed signs of being when he arrived.'

Appleby stared at Clandon thoughtfully. 'That wouldn't be because of your playing down the possible calamitousness of the thing?'

'Certainly not. It was my idea that it might brace brother Miles to be told straight just what the conceivable stakes were. I put it in the same entirely untechnical language that I treated you to, my dear Appleby, when this bombshell first burst on us. We have all sorts of checks and precautions at our little game, and according to the book of rules I ought to have known, day by day, precisely what Howard was, or was not, in possession of. But Howard is far too brilliant – and wayward, if you like – to stick to all that. So, when he vanished, I was in no position to check up with certainty. Supposing him to have been quite, quite mad – which we are agreed is one possible starting point – then he *may* conceivably have had it in his power to walk out with something almost inconceivably lethal. I put that to brother Miles straight.'

'And how did he react?'

'Reasonably enough. He asked me for my own opinion – my own estimate of the degree of probability that it was such a situation we are up against. I gave him my own honest answer: that there's a slight balance of probability against Howard's being in possession of anything of the sort.'

Appleby frowned. 'I see. Well – that's why Miles' nervous tone has improved. He has confidence in your opinion – which is the only well-informed one, after all.'

'Perhaps so. At the time, I was chiefly struck by his inability to make much of it all. No doubt he's a classical man, and all that. But his ability to grasp some elementary scientific conceptions is pretty dim. I doubt whether he understood the nature of a filter-passing virus.'

'Didn't he, indeed?' Appleby had turned away rather absently, and was once more studying the Thames. 'But Miles' intellectual constitution is less relevant than Howard's emotional one. That's what I want to get clearer from you, Clandon. What I *have* got doesn't help. I mean that, in a way, I'd like to think of Howard as a bit battier than you seem able to bring him out.'

'I understand that – and, mind you, Howard's a dark horse. Although I've worked with him so closely for some time, there are few men I'm conscious of being so uncertain about. Of course he lives on his nerves, as so many top-flighters do. He's a worrying type, in a way. But then so does brother Miles seem to be – so that's perhaps no more than a family trait.'

Appleby reflected for a moment. 'But I gather you don't suspect Howard of regarding the whole drift of his work as a nightmare?'

'Well, no – not quite that. Of course, he does brood at times on the insane purposes science is being harnessed to. We all do that. And I've known him, in phases of discouragement, declare our own particular position – at the research station, I mean – to be on the verge of becoming morally impossible and unendurable. But then he bobs up again, damns all governments roundly, and says that we'll whack some sense into them yet. By "us" he means, you know, scientists as a class – or as a calling or vocation or whatever. If I have doubts about Howard having cracked up and gone batty, it's because of that intensity of faith in "us". No doubt, if something happened to undermine that faith, he'd be in for a bad time.'

'But, so far as you know, nothing has?'

Clandon nodded emphatically. 'So far as I know, nothing has. Rather the contrary. In June he went to a conference in Amsterdam, and met some top Russians. He came back quite cheered up. Those chaps, he said, were pretty cautious, of course. But it was clear that, in a last analysis, they belonged to "us" one hundred per cent.'

'Not meaning more, really, than that they are good and sincere scientists?'

'Oh, quite so. Still, Howard was rather cheered up, as I say. Although worried, at the same time, by the whole damned thing.' Clandon shook his head impatiently. 'I find it hard to give you the picture of Howard as I see or feel it. Comes of being no sort of psychologist, I suppose.'

Appleby smiled. 'Aren't you simply saying this: that your Head Man has been at times sorely troubled, but has shown no signs of really acute anxiety?'

'That's it.' Clandon looked relieved. 'That's it exactly. No acute anxiety. Except, conceivably, about his brother.'

'What's that you say?' For a moment Appleby was left staring. 'I'm quite clear that *Miles* has been subject to rather acute anxiety about *Howard*: about his brother's whole moral position and so on. Are you telling me that *Howard* has been in acute anxiety about *Miles*?'

'Well, yes – I am, as a matter of fact.' Clandon was almost apologetic. 'Mind you, Howard hasn't often talked to me about Miles. And, when he has, his overt attitude hasn't been of anxiety at all. He's professed rather to envy Miles his obscure and blameless life. You can imagine the sort of thing: decent job teaching decent boys decency. Not, like ourselves, walking a razor's edge between science and lunacy. Obvious line. Wholesome line, for that matter. I take it about my own elder brother, who's happy all the year round, just improving the estate and chasing foxes.'

'Bother your own elder brother.' Appleby was almost excited. 'What has seemed to lie under Howard's obvious line?'

'The notion, I imagine, that Miles is thoroughly unstable. And it's so strong in Howard, if you ask me, that it has to peep out whenever Miles is in focus at all.'

'A kind of morbid apprehensiveness?'

'My dear chap, you do put these things well. Comes of constantly having to size people up, I suppose.' Clandon seemed genuinely admiring. 'Put it this way: if Howard read of something pretty calamitous happening to somebody, he'd be apt to think that that's just the sort of thing likely to happen to Miles. A foreboding attitude, you might say. And occasionally sticking out so that even a mere nose-in-test-tube type like myself must notice it. Brotherly instinct for protectiveness, I suppose.'

'No doubt it can be put that way. And I'm no sort of psychologist either. But wouldn't it be orthodox psychoanalytical doctrine that the basis of such an attitude – at least if at all obsessive – lies in deep unconscious hostility?'

Clandon was silent for a moment. 'Deep waters,' he said quietly. 'And I suppose Cain and Abel are latent in every pair of brothers. But identical twins may be a special case. Probably one pundit would regard them as one sort of special case, and another would regard them as another. Meanwhile, where do we go? Unconscious hostility is a queer notion to take up – having landed ourselves with the fantastic situation we have.'

'I couldn't agree more.' Appleby paced the room. 'So take it, for a start, in terms of common sense. Excessive anxiety about a brother – or any other relative – would be too pathological altogether if there weren't some reasonable springboard for it. Well, I suppose Miles might be said to afford something of the sort?'

'I wonder.' Clandon hesitated. 'Do you know, I don't think much of it? Remember that our only experience of brother Miles is in a thoroughly upsetting context. First, you go down and tell him his brother's vanished. And second, he's yanked off to undertake a decidedly queer assignment. Well, he's had his bad time, as I've described. But it's not clear to me that in any circumstances he'd be a really bad risk. Would you agree?'

Appleby, back at the window, was watching a line of lighters dropping down river. 'Well, yes. Only – ' He broke off impatiently. 'But bother Miles! He's only the stand-in, after all; and we're allowing him to become a blasted red herring. I rather wish I'd let him alone. And I bet you do.'

Clandon rumbled amiably. 'I can take it, my dear fellow. Incidentally, I suppose I'd better be getting back. I'm principal stage-manager, after all.' He hesitated for a moment. 'You've thought of straightforward abduction – plain violence? We live amid so much blessed law and order that perhaps we tend – '

'Yes, indeed.' Appleby interrupted at once impatiently and with perfect good humour. 'If morbid psychology is being kept well in view, it isn't to the exclusion of simple melodrama. In fact, at the moment, it's on melodrama that I'd put my money.'

But after all – Appleby said to himself when Clandon had gone – need my money be on melodrama either? It's a possibility, it's a definite field I have a dozen men working on now – but am I missing the likeliest explanation of the lot? And just because I've been stampeded into taking the sensational view? The PM perturbed and informing the Cabinet. My own Minister wanting to guard the reservoirs. The genuinely alarming thought of how the public might react to a bit of scare reporting. *Bacillus botulinus* has already been making some headway in people's imaginations. Suppose the populace at large got the idea that any wandering stranger of intellectual appearance was likely to be the mad scientist, intent on dropping the small fatal dose straight into the national teapot? It is a prospect almost equally ugly whether false or true.

And – just conceivably – it *is* true, more or less. But it is far more probably false. So, too, are all the other more sensational readings of the affair. Isn't it likely, in fact, to be on a par with two or three other cases with which I've been concerned in the last half-dozen years?

Marchbanks, for instance – remember him. He hadn't been kidnapped. He hadn't gone mad. He hadn't even bolted with somebody else's wife. He had simply packed a bag and gone off trout-fishing in Scotland. And, although Marchbanks' disappearance was public property from the first, with a national hue and cry whipped up by twopenny papers, nobody came within a mile of spotting him for a month. Marchbanks himself had read *The Scotsman* every day over his tea, and without himself turning a hair. He was just being damned to them – which was an expression, come to think of it, that the Junipers seemed to be fond of as a family. Marchbanks – so far as Appleby could make out afterwards – hadn't as much as seen the thing as an enormous joke. His absence had cost no end of public money; heaven knew what complicated experiment had gone to pot because of it; but the simple fact was that he had decided it was about time for a holiday.

And wasn't Howard Juniper – Professor Howard Juniper – out of the same stable: a don, seconded to this national work, who had grown up in an ancient university as a sweet law unto himself? Appleby would never forget the mild surprise with which Marchbanks, run to earth – or rather run to burn – in Morayshire, had received the suggestion that there might be people who were displeased with him. He'd had more useful ideas, he'd said, while flogging this very decent bit of water, than he'd had for years in their ineptly pretentious laboratories. He'd even brought off the really crucial experiment at last – with a length of gut, Mrs Macnabb's porridge pan, and a really superb spring-trap that old Macnabb had invented in pursuance of his profession as a poacher. So what the hell?

Appleby smiled at the memory. There was decidedly a lesson in Marchbanks. Entirely sane, Marchbanks had been, even if by some standards irresponsible.

Irresponsible… The word moved uneasily in Appleby's mind. It was something that Miles Juniper had said. It was something in the tone, the mere inflexion, of something he had said… Appleby paused on this, aware that he was on curiously obscure ground. For this hadn't been the only moment of its kind during that interview at Splaine Croft. There had been something else of the sort too: something that had just hung for a moment on the ear – and something that Appleby, try as he might, just couldn't pinpoint or bring back to consciousness. But *this* was clear enough. Miles had expressed his certainty that his brother Howard was up to nothing irresponsible. But there had been just the faintest hesitation or reservation in the way he had said it.

And there was that freakish past – common, indeed to both brothers. Wasn't it conceivable that Howard Juniper had simply behaved in some fashion that would indeed be merely freakish in an unimportant young man, but that did rather more than verge upon irresponsibility in a famous one?

Very well. Go back to Marchbanks. He had in the end found Marchbanks – and had put a good deal of ingenuity into the task. But wouldn't he have done it quicker if he had kept one fact more clearly in focus from the start? When a man bolts from his job it is probably because he is fed up with it. And the natural thing to do, when one is fed up with one's job, is to turn to one's hobbies. Dry-fly fishing had been Marchbanks' hobby. What about Howard Juniper's? Drop for the moment – Appleby said to himself – all the more sinister pictures this business has conjured up. See if you can get anywhere with the simple notion of a chap bolting to have a go at something he is known to like.

He reached for one among the several neat files that the Juniper affair was bringing to his desk every day. It was the one that began with Howard Juniper's entry in *Who's Who* and went on to as complete a biographical outline as could be built up. When he reread it carefully he pressed a bell on his desk.

'You see *that*?' he said to the secretary who answered it – and pointed to a place on the page. 'What do you think of the possibility of our missing friend's having gone harking back to something of the sort?'

'Not much,' the secretary said promptly.

'Nor I. Would you say it would be a good time of year for it?'

'Nice weather, and all that, sir. But I really haven't a clue. Get an expert view, of course, in ten minutes.'

Appleby nodded. 'Go ahead. It's another of those tiresome stones.'

'Not to be left unturned, sir? Quite so.' The secretary, who was young and alert, nodded cheerfully.

'And find out about the most likely place where this sort of interest' – Appleby tapped his file again – 'may be – um – prosecuted.'

'Certainly, sir. Anything else?'

'Yes, Charles. Just see if you can get me Judith on the telephone.'

Two minutes later the instrument purred on the desk. 'Lady Appleby on the line, sir,' a voice said.

'Judith – is that you?'

'Of course it's me. Aren't you coming home to lunch?'

'No, I'm not. And I want you to make yours a sandwich in the car. Do you think that you could – entirely unobtrusively – do a job that normally requires quite a large squad of police?'

'I imagine so.' Judith Appleby sounded entirely unsurprised. 'But just what's the idea? A tardy thought at Scotland Yard about saving the taxpayer's money?'

Appleby laughed. 'There's that aspect to it, no doubt. But it's not precisely what's in my mind. Listen.'

'Go ahead,' Judith said.

3

Judith Appleby, as it happened, had heard of Splaine Croft. Two of her friends had sent sons there, and had reported with satisfaction that it seemed a fairly civilized sort of place. It was funny how, as civilization seeped away, the idea of civilization became all the go. She rather distrusted it. People now said 'a civilized chap' where she herself would have been prompted to say 'rather a smooth type'. Certainly to go looking for civilized boarding-schools for one's young was dangerous, even if laudable. If what you insisted on were the old-fashioned desiderata: gravel soil, southern exposure, all-Oxford staff, toughening them up, licking them into shape, rubbing off the awkward corners – if you were after these and similar prescriptive futilities and iniquities, you were at least pretty sure of getting what you looked for; and, if you were eccentric enough to want something else, you kept the kids at home. But if you went round looking for civilization, you were only too likely to get heaven knew what...

Still, reasonable friends had praised Splaine Croft. Judith therefore drove up to it in a mood of only modified prejudice. She was acquiescing in more or less orthodox education for her own young; and it couldn't be said that they showed any marked ill-effects so far. But having herself been brought up at home, in a large house full of assorted relations who were mostly mad, and having found this interesting and entirely satisfactory, she was always ready to take a poor view of what she called institutions.

Splaine Croft – she noted contentedly as she drew up the car – looked unappealing on a day of warm thundery summer rain. John had reported liking the place – but John was capable of liking

50

anything that was really efficiently run. And no doubt Splaine Croft was that. The windows were clean; they were also blank and uncurtained and thus doubtless let in more light. There was a garden to one side, crammed with roses – but probably only the headmaster was allowed into it. Straight in front of the main entrance stood a flagstaff. Clearly the boys were paraded round it on appropriate occasions for the purpose of singing *God Save the Queen.* Hanging in the hall there would be a certificate praising the drains. And the headmaster's study would be protected by a supernumerary green-baize door, to muffle the howling when the headmaster's pupils were being caned. Upstairs in the dormitories the most prominent furnishing would be a profusion of rope-ladders designed to assuage the anxieties of prospective parents apprehensive of fire. But in term-time these would be firmly padlocked to the wall, since what the headmaster himself was apprehensive of was any too ready means to suicide. Yes – Judith said to herself firmly – I have been here before. I can smell the disinfectant. I can slip on the tiles. I can extract, from the pitch-pine panelling of the interior, small gouts of resinous substance that can be satisfactorily rolled between finger and thumb. And that is sometimes the only resource through long weary hours.

'Can I help you to find anybody?'

A small boy in a blue windcheater, running past in the rain, had wheeled and come politely to a halt by the open window of Judith's car.

One of the extra-unfortunates, Judith thought, who have to stay through the holidays as well. A dozen or so boys altogether, John said. Afterwards, I wonder, could I offer to take them all out to tea? Aloud she said – thereby beginning the course of duplicity she was much looking forward to – 'Can you tell me if Mr Juniper is about?'

'The Head's had to go away to a funeral. Isn't it a bore?'

'Well, yes – I don't suppose he finds it invigorating.'

The small boy smiled charmingly at being trusted to understand this long word. 'No, I don't mean that. A bore that he isn't here I mean. Of course, Pooh and Piglet are all right – '

'Pooh and Piglet?' The unfortunate waifs, Judith supposed, got through their weary days partly by a relapse upon nursery fantasy.

'Oh, just a couple of undergraduates we have to cope with. They're very decent really. Last night we absolutely soaked them with our water jugs, and they gave us a wonderful scragging afterwards. But, of course, doing nothing but larking around is rather a waste of time. The point about the Head – I expect you've heard – is his leg break. You see, *he can teach it*. He really can. If you're prepared to work hard at it, that's to say. And I think I really was getting it, and so were Alabaster Two and U-Tin, and now the Head's gone off to this funeral, and it's going to absorb him for days.'

'That seems too bad.'

'And, you see, all three of us are going to different public schools. U-Tin is going to Eton – everybody with a name like that does, you know – and I'm going to Radley, and Alabaster Two is going to Downside because he's a Jew.'

'A Jew?' Judith asked doubtfully.

'Or is it a Catholic? Anyway, the point is that we can all take the same leg break to different schools. You see? But I'm being a frightful bore. Can I find you somebody else? Pooh or Piglet? Piglet's less shy, I'd say. Or there's Miss Grimstone, the secretary. She's not shy at all.'

'I think Miss Grimstone will be best. You see' – Judith looked with limpid candour at the small boy – 'I'm thinking of sending my sons here. Kevin and Jerry.'

'Can they swim?'

'Yes, they swim quite well. For people' – Judith added with proper humility – 'still at baby school, that's to say.'

'Well, it's really not bad.' The small boy offered this as one who considers a large complexity of balanced factors. 'Only get some of their friends – small boys they know quite well, and who won't frighten them – to toss them in a blanket a bit before you send them. It makes the first night easier. All the chaps whose families are in the know about Splaine arrange for that.'

'Thank you,' Judith said. She was much encouraged by this glimpse of savagery. 'And is your headmaster a really nice man?'

The small boy frowned. He probably doubted this question's being quite good form. Nevertheless he answered with continued frankness. 'He's terribly decent, really. Of course, he does seem a disappointed man. It makes him restless. We think he must have been frightfully ambitious. And, of course, it didn't come off.'

'Ambitious?' Judith found this interesting.

'He was a Rugger Cap, you know, which ought to satisfy any man. But, at the same time, he had this natural leg break. So he hoped to play for England as a cricketer too. It would have been unique, almost. But he just didn't bring it off.' Judith's informant shook his head seriously. 'We think that's what messed him up.'

'Messed – ' Judith checked herself as she saw the boy, for the first time, shift rather uneasily from one foot to the other. 'But look, you're getting frightfully wet. Do just take me in to Miss Grimstone.'

Left in charge of Splaine Croft, Miss Grimstone received visitors in the drawing-room. Judith looked round it with interest. It was the sort of entirely feminine and decidedly old-fashioned apartment which some bachelors think proper to keep about the house in pious memory of a mother.

But it was a pleasant room in itself – and no doubt there would be prospective parents over whom its selling-power could be considerable. Gentlefolk have to be on the job for a good many generations, Judith reflected, to build up just this sort of everything-good and everything-faded effect. The bits and pieces of French furniture had really come from France – and already long ago local carpenters had had to be called in to remedy unfortunate disintegrations. The few watercolours were really by Girtin and Paul Sandby and the elder and the younger Cozens, and they had been acquired by Junipers when such things cost a good deal less than they do now. The whole room was much of a piece – the only odd note being struck by a modern portrait-bust in bronze. Judith, being a sculptor herself, saw at a glance who it was by. Fifteen hundred guineas, she said to herself. And then Miss Grimstone entered the room.

Judith shook hands and then turned to the large bay window. It looked out on the rose garden. 'Peace!' she said enthusiastically.

Miss Grimstone peered at her intently through thick lenses. 'It is,' she admitted, 'a secluded situation.'

'No – those roses. The large yellow ones with the faint pink flush. Peace. Such a beautiful name for a rose. Do you know' – and Judith turned impulsively to Miss Grimstone – 'I am quite, quite sure that Kevin and Jerry would be very, very happy here!'

'And they might even learn something, if that is judged to be of any importance.' Miss Grimstone, who regarded Splaine Croft not as a refuge from the miseries of the world but as a place at which there were standards to keep up, clearly had no scruple about snubbing gush. 'And how curious, Lady Appleby, that your sons would appear to be named out of *Finnegans Wake.*'

Judith felt a sinking sensation inside. She was the more disconcerted because Miss Grimstone had so unmistakably the appearance of one whose literary studies are unlikely to have proceeded beyond *Eric,* or *Little by Little.* Irresponsible humour, clearly, ought not to be cultivated by those who would assist Scotland Yard.

'*Finnegans Wake!*' she said, perplexed. 'Is that quite a *nice* book?'

'Since it is largely unintelligible, the point is hard to determine. No doubt the matter of your children's names is coincidental.'

'Of course,' Judith said, 'my husband's family are Irish.'

'Indeed? You surprise me, Lady Appleby. To my mind, the name has Yorkshire associations.'

'Quite so. The Cromwellian Settlement, you know, Miss Grimstone. How useful history is! Kevin and Jerry both adore it.'

Miss Grimstone, although receiving this last assertion with undisguised scepticism, was obviously impressed by the suggestion of Applebys busy in a territorial way in the seventeenth century. 'I am sure,' she said, 'that Mr Juniper would wish me to tell you that the prospect of any vacancies in the near future is very small. We are almost fully booked up for some years ahead. Most boys who come to Splaine are either sons of old Splaine boys or have had elder brothers at the school. A certain priority has to be accorded to applications in which there are circumstances of that kind. But I am sure that Mr Juniper would do his best. Would your husband have been born in Kilkenny?'

'No, not Kilkenny.' Judith, who knew very well that John had been born at Kirkby Overblow, was disconcerted by this. 'In Wicklow. But Appleby House is now a ruin, unfortunately. It was burnt down in the troubles.'

'How very shocking.' Miss Grimstone was again discernibly impressed. 'I ask simply because we have a closed scholarship for boys coming from Kilkenny. Wicklow, I'm afraid, wouldn't count. And now, I think you may care to look over part of the school? Both matron and housekeeper are unfortunately on holiday, but I think I can tell you enough, perhaps, about the domestic side.'

'Oh, thank you *so* much.' Judith felt it was now incumbent upon her to think up the sort of questions and attitudes proper in one who has married into the Irish landed gentry. 'You have your own green vegetables, I suppose?'

'Most certainly. Everything of that sort is grown within the grounds.'

'And cows?'

'Of course. We have' – Miss Grimstone spoke without a flicker – 'special cows, suitable for invalids, infants, and young and tender stomachs in general.'

'That is most satisfactory.' Judith had an uneasy feeling that Miss Grimstone, too, was capable of indulging obscure and unseasonable humour. 'And now I would certainly like to see over the school.'

'The house is a large and rambling one, as you will have noticed, Lady Appleby. But I can certainly show you over the greater part of the boys' quarters. And the kitchens – which are, of course, most important.'

Judith had certainly noticed the size of the house. John had given her a decidedly tall order. Wondering what was to be done about it, she let her glance stray once more round the drawing-room. It came to rest on the bronze bust.

'Is that,' she asked suddenly, 'a bust of Mr Juniper's famous brother?'

Miss Grimstone didn't take this inquiry very well. 'The bust,' she said severely, 'is of Mr Juniper himself.'

'Oh, I see! Commissioned, no doubt, by old pupils of the school.'

'I think not.' Miss Grimstone, although disapproving this curiosity, was allowing herself a tone that was faintly dry. 'If you are interested in contemporary art, Lady Appleby, I must show you the Augustus John in the dining-room.'

'Of Mr Juniper again? Not delivering his celebrated leg break?'

'I think,' Miss Grimstone said, 'we might begin with the chapel. It is all that remains of the house formerly standing on the site. We are very proud of it. There is some fine modern glass. Which *was* presented by old boys.'

I must take it for granted – Judith said to herself as she went peering here and there in the interest of the mythical Kevin and Jerry – that the missing scientist is on the premises. He has committed a crime, he has done something disgraceful, he has gone harmlessly off his head. Anything that would prompt his schoolmastering brother to say, 'Very well, lie low here for a time.' That is the situation, and when John popped up here the other day the unfortunate schoolmaster was taken completely by surprise, and could do nothing but acquiesce in his plan. Alternatively, what is lurking here now is not Professor Howard Juniper living but Professor Howard Juniper dead. His brother has done him in. An affair of passion connected, no doubt, with Miss Grimstone. And my dear husband has pleasantly given me the task of finding the body. A policeman's wife is not a happy one.

Outside, it was still raining dismally, and thunder was rumbling in the distance. And everything was planned for outside at this time of the year, so that there was a feeling abroad that the day was running drearily down. In one empty classroom the boy who had chattered so cheerfully to Judith on her arrival was now forlornly engaged in sticking together the parts of a model aeroplane which obviously bored him extremely. U-Tin – it was easy to identify U-Tin – was in a corner of the boys' day-room, addressing himself with equal lack of conviction to a chess problem. Alabaster Two – since he was in blue corduroy he was presumably Alabaster Two – was in another corner, playing ludo with a conscientiously interested young man who must be either Pooh or Piglet. The holiday boarders ran about uncertainly; and Piglet (if the ludo-player was Pooh) kept on rounding them up and making suggestions of which they didn't think too well.

Judith, conscious of this state of affairs as Miss Grimstone marched her around, found herself suddenly in the possession of a plan. It would be exhausting, but it might work very well. Unfortunately there was one serious difficulty in the way of putting it into operation. She herself hadn't arrived at Splaine as quite the right person. Gushing and enthusiastic, yes. But not quite *jolly* enough. That was it… Judith, as Miss Grimstone showed her the kitchens and the up-to-date refrigeration, set herself to modulate, unobtrusively but rapidly, into a very jolly person indeed. An admiral's daughter, she said to herself. A Betjeman girl. Or a matron from Eliot's land of lobelias and tennis flannels. Slap Miss Grimstone on the back? Well, not quite. It was important to be asked to stay to tea.

A bell clanged out somewhere above the domestic offices. It was a cracked bell, Judith noted, of the kind with which the sombre imagination of Graham Greene regularly provides schools in the distressful memories of his male characters. But at Splaine Croft this horror of the ringing bell (John Donne, Judith told herself, being thus launched upon literary references) appeared to be rather cheerfully received. Perhaps it was because it did, on this occasion, mean tea. There was a general stampede to the dining hall.

'Are they to have tea?' Judith asked – enthusiastic and oh so jolly. 'But I *must* see them! May I just peep?'

'During the holidays I myself take tea with the school.' Miss Grimstone glanced at Judith with what could not be other than naked suspicion. 'I hope you have time to take a cup yourself? It is far from elegant, of course. But thoroughly wholesome. Each boy has half a pint of milk from the special cows.'

Judith found herself wondering what this formidable old person really believed about her. That she was some brazen woman from a magazine, perhaps, preparing a colourful feature on the education of the surtax-paying classes. Still, here she was safely in the dining hall, where Pooh and Piglet were being introduced to her under perfectly commonplace names that she didn't catch. At school, of course, small boys are not introduced. But Judith, considering it to be all in her part, shook hands with them all vigorously. They stared at her, polite but round-eyed. She acknowledged in herself a flickering suspicion that she was not a terribly good actress. Everybody sat down at a single long table at one end of the room. The panelling, she noticed, wasn't pitch pine, but some really gloomy high-class stuff. A city gent's house, once upon a time, Splaine Croft must have been.

In the absence of the school matron, Miss Grimstone poised the beautiful Georgian teapot from which the grown-ups were to recruit themselves. Her aged features took on an inquiring expression, so that Judith supposed she was about to say, 'Sugar and cream?'

'I didn't gather' – this was what Miss Grimstone actually asked – 'whether Kevin and Jerry are twins?'

'Well, *almost* twins.'

There was a pained silence. Pooh and Piglet gave each other a quick apprehensive glance, as if doubting the propriety rather than the credibility of this obscure obstetrical intelligence. Judith improved the occasion by a large jolly laugh. Miss Grimstone refrained from further interrogation. U-Tin, who was presumably some sort of prince, made a few polite remarks in an English that was faultless but perhaps a little too formal for his years. The other boys ate mostly in silence; the rain still streaming down outside the windows made them glum. Judith, thus left with a clear field, offered the company a breezy account of her childhood. Her father, although perpetually afloat as admirals always are, had kept his family in the heart of the countryside. A large family, Judith explained, in a large rambling house. Really very like Splaine Croft.

'Did it have secret passages?' Alabaster Two asked suddenly.

'Well, no – but there were very deep cellars.'

'My grandfather's place has secret passages,' Alabaster Two said. And added modestly: 'But, of course, it's a sort of castle, and you'd expect them.'

'Secret passages are best, I agree,' Judith said. 'But having several staircases is important too. With two staircases you can have very decent hide-and-seek. But with *three* staircases – '

'Splaine has three staircases,' the boy who had first encountered Judith interrupted.

'Has it really?' Judith seemed not to have made herself aware of this fact. 'Well, with *three* staircases you can play Chinese Torturers.'

There was a moment of impressed silence. Judith's credit had mounted perceptibly. She might perhaps be a person really entitled to that sort of laugh.

'Chinese Torturers?' Piglet asked with interest. He was a pleasant lad, Judith thought, but with a mental age probably a good deal below U-Tin's. 'I don't think it's in the Weekend Book.'

'It certainly isn't.' Judith rejected this suggestion with civil scorn. 'It's the sort of game that is known only in a very few families. It was known in mine. We also knew Hungry Tigers. And Heads Off Quick. But Chinese Torturers was the best.'

Miss Grimstone alone seemed to react unfavourably to this. 'The title,' she said, 'fails to commend itself to me, I confess. I hope it was not a game that carried any suggestion of cruelty, or gave scope for bullying.'

'Well, of course, you have to *imagine* the most frightful things.' Judith was concerned to be fair-minded. 'And there is *lots* of rough and tumble.'

'I would suppose,' Miss Grimstone said drily, 'that Kevin and Jerry would not care for it at all. Although it *is* a family game.'

'And it's the most splendid exercise' – Judith ignored this shaft – 'for a wet day. You rush all over *and over* the house. That's where the staircases come in.'

'It sounds tremendous fun,' Pooh said. He looked cautiously at Judith, plainly indulging a callow vision of the fun that a little rough and tumble in her company might produce. Judith smiled at him brightly. Not so nice as Piglet, she was thinking. He reads too many modern novels, full of accessible women and inexpressible men.

'Could you tell us the rules, please?' U-Tin said politely.

'Well, of course, there are two sides: victims and executioners.' Judith frowned. 'I'm afraid it's rather hard to *explain*. But if I could just *show* you – '

It was a suggestion perfectly timed. The remaining mugs of milk from the special cows were drained at a gulp and amid general clamour. Even Miss Grimstone made no protest when Judith – by what she thought was her most brilliant stroke – suggested that the secretary's office should be the den.

Not very surprisingly, Chinese Torturers proved to be very hard work – the more so as Judith had the task of improvising the rules as they went along. But at least she had one perfectly clear guiding principle: everybody must go rushing about everywhere, and in sufficient excitement not to notice that her own rushing about was on more systematic lines. When she had explained that she herself was the crucial personage called the Mandarin, that the Mandarin hurried around all the time, and that sundry penalties attended this dread figure's spotting either executioners or victims, she found that she had got the situation pretty well under control. Even Pooh was no difficulty, since his libidinousness was unsupported by the resolution necessary to the making of any progress from fantasy towards fact. Nor was the game hampered, as she had feared might be the case, by any disposition to regard parts of Splaine Croft as sacrosanct or out of bounds. The boys romped as cheerfully in the drawing-room or in Miles Juniper's study as they did in their own dormitories or day-rooms. It was a genuinely uninhibited place. Rather more surprising was the fact that Miss Grimstone proved uninhibited too – to the extent of appointing herself Chief Executioner out of hand and stumping short-sightedly about with a great deal of gusto.

It took Judith more than an hour of Chinese Torturers to feel that she had been thoroughly all over the place. A modern preparatory school, it seemed, had to make provision for other activities than

Latin, Maths, and Cricket. There was quite an elaborately fitted out theatre. There was a large art room, crammed with materials for painting, modelling, and carving, and with a surprising collection of plaster casts of nondescript Roman emperors and classical gods and goddesses. There was a full-sized horse that came to bits for the purpose, it appeared, of anatomical study. Television sets, radios, gramophones, tape-recorders, and cinematograph apparatus lurked in corners and cupboards. Education seemed to have become very complicated. And it must be decidedly expensive.

The outbuildings constituted a distinct problem – and this might have remained insoluble if it had gone on raining. But in fact the rain had stopped and only the thunder was growling a little nearer, with now and then a flicker of lightning against an overcast sky. Judith began to feel curiously uneasy. Either it was the electricity in the air, or there was an element of strain she hadn't at first recognized in all this scampering about in the vague expectation of hitting upon something sinister. Could there really be a living man lurking in the house, unknown to all these lively and curious children? She was almost sure there couldn't be, and that she had eliminated what was an improbable speculation from the first. But, of course, a live man didn't exhaust the possibilities. And she really must manage to do the outbuildings. They were extensive, but all grouped more or less together to form a large stable-yard.

Her problem was solved by the boys themselves. Quite suddenly, as if they possessed some paranormal means of communication such as is said to govern the evolutions of a flock of birds, they had abandoned the game she had invented for them, and poured out into the open air. They were now playing a game of their own, which somebody told her in a shout to be Cowboys and Red Indians. As she now had no share in directing their proceedings, she had correspondingly no further plausible status among them; and she saw that she couldn't, without blank eccentricity, continue for more than a few minutes longer to wander gamesomely around. Pooh and Piglet had disappeared. Perhaps it was an hour at which their university studies claimed them. Miss Grimstone had returned to her more settled character as school secretary, and would certainly be expecting Judith to clear out, It was quite a long run back to London, and by this time Kevin and Jerry ought to be wondering what had happened to Mummy.

But she could cover the remaining ground in ten minutes, if she simply walked firmly and frankly from building to building and briskly raked through each. And the moment was suddenly favourable – for Miss Grimstone was called away to the telephone, and had excused herself with a hint of understandable impatience. Judith went rapidly to work.

The largest building had been converted into a gym. She had already stuck her head into it when being shown round; it was perfectly reasonable that she should have a better look now. And this didn't take two minutes. It had once been a stable with a loft above. But the floor of the loft had been removed and it was open to the roof, with ropes and rope-ladders hanging from the exposed beams. Finding this totally unrewarding, Judith emerged again into the open air. For an August early evening it had gone strangely dark, so that a flicker of lightning that met her as she came out was almost theatrically effective. Somewhere she could hear some of the boys shouting, and among them she thought she could distinguish the particularly precise tones of U-Tin. But the yard itself was now deserted. She walked past a row of empty stalls, peering in. They no longer kept ponies at Splaine Croft, she had been told. Riding must be an 'extra' that no longer much commended itself to small boys. Which was, of course, deplorable –

Judith found that she had halted abruptly, and with a quickened pulse. For a moment she had no idea why. Then she realized that it was because she had heard a low moan. A growl of thunder, a low moan, and then a growl of thunder again… Only the moan wasn't a moan; it was nothing more out of the way than a half-open door on one of the stalls turning on a rusty hinge.

It was absurd. It was absurd that, hard upon romping round with all these children, she should be abruptly playing nervous tricks with herself. Partly, no doubt, it was the sudden solitude – for now the voices were quite far away, as if everybody had moved off across the playing fields. If they had, they might get soaked at any time, for certainly anything could come tumbling out of that extraordinary sky. She herself would probably have to drive home through a tremendous storm. And the sooner the better. For she did now very much want to get away from Splaine. It was, beyond almost any suspicion, a thoroughly harmless place. Indeed, it was a genuinely jolly place – which made her own spuriously jolly act only the more uncomfortable in retrospect. But she would have a look at the last remaining building, all the same.

It was almost the twin of the one that had been turned into a gym. For a moment she thought the door was locked – which was odd, since at Splaine locks and keys seemed virtually not to exist. But it was only stiff. She pushed harder, and found herself looking into a large dark, empty space. Or almost empty. It was used as a store for miscellaneous sports equipment. Rugger posts, waiting to be put up again for next term. A pile of hurdles. Some coils of rope. A sight screen, dismantled and in need of repair. She could just distinguish these objects as her eyes got accustomed to the gloom. Then suddenly, as if directly behind her, there was the first really vivid flash of lightning. It served simply to reveal the place definitively as entirely innocent.

She was about to turn when it occurred to her to look upwards. There was a murky plaster ceiling here, which meant that there must be some sort of loft or garret up above. But nothing seemed to give access to it, and she supposed there must be an outside staircase on the farther side of the building. Then the lightning came again. And she saw a large square hole in the ceiling, close to the opposite wall. She moved cautiously through the near-darkness that followed the flash. Yes – there must have been a wooden staircase going up that way. But it had been removed. She explored more carefully. The signs of something of the kind were obvious. The staircase had been rather roughly torn down.

There was really nothing suspicious, she thought, about that. Probably it had become unsafe, and had been cut away to keep the boys from getting into mischief on it. Judith hesitated. It was almost certain that up there she would find nothing but cobwebs, unless indeed it was an owl or a colony of bats. And yet, that loft was unique. It was the only place in Splaine that was not entirely accessible to anybody who cared to wander about.

She went back into the yard. Everything was warm and steamy and still, and there was a long lull in the thunder. She glanced towards the gym. She knew very well what she was looking for: a ladder that she had noticed out of the corner of her eye. Yes, there it was, lying on the ground not twenty yards away. It would probably reach. And it looked reasonably light.

She was burning her boats as any normal sort of visitor. If Miss Grimstone returned and found her stumping across the yard carrying a ladder, she would probably judge her so mad that it would be advisable to send for the police. Which would be embarrassing – particularly for John. Judith was still meditating this when she found that she had in fact secured the thing and was staggering back with it. This part of the proceeding was fairly easy. Getting the ladder more or less perpendicular and so up to the hole in the ceiling was another matter. But she remembered how to do it. You got one end above your head and then walked towards the other end, shifting your hands from rung to rung.

This proved not too difficult either. It seemed only a couple of minutes before she was actually climbing. Would there – she wondered – be a skylight? She hadn't a torch. Not even a box of matches. Which was inefficient. She should have taken thought.

But now her head was through the hole. And there was light – of sorts. It seemed to come from a single narrow window at a gable-end, and was almost negligible, with the sky as it now was. She climbed the remaining rungs and stepped cautiously on to the floor. For there *was* a floor. And it seemed to support every variety of junk. The place was precisely what one might expect it to be: a very large lumber-room. And the lumber was of an order so utterly useless that the staircase had been dismantled with no thought to it. Judith had just decided that this was the particular anticlimax to this part of her adventure when the lightning came again – and this time there was a terrific clap of thunder straight above her head.

Afterwards, she blamed that thunder a good deal. It was so immensely louder than anything that had preceded it that it took her entirely by surprise. It had never in her life occurred to her to be frightened by thunder – and now she was uncertain that she wasn't suddenly weak at the knees. It's absurd, she told herself again. I don't behave like this. And suddenly she told herself: *There's a horrible smell.*

Feeling her way past packing-cases full and empty, past a grotesque hatstand, past mouldering trunks, empty picture frames, an old hip-bath – feeling her way past these, moving desperately forward simply so that she shouldn't ignominiously bolt, she said to herself: *Things do die in places like this.* And she added, trying to get it definite: *Even a pigeon doesn't always just shrivel up.*

She turned a corner – round some shapeless stuffed affair that might have been an abandoned vaulting-horse. It was darker. It was quite dark. Her actions had become senseless. She wasn't conducting a hunt any more. She wasn't sure she wasn't being hunted. And suddenly she stumbled – perhaps it was over a curtain rod or a hockey stick. Falling forward, she put out her hand to save herself – and suddenly knew that she had clasped another hand. But the hand returned no grip of its own; it was rigid and cold. Then there was a long instant of blinding light and she was looking at a man's face: cold and rigid and very, very white. This time, when the thunder crashed, it seemed to be actually inside the loft with her and rattling at the roof in a maniacal effort to get free.

She struggled up from hands and knees – to realize that somebody was standing close behind her. It was a man. She made a tremendous effort to turn and face him. But before she could manage it, the man spoke.

'Oh, I say, Lady Appleby, what awful fun!'

It was the young man the boys called Pooh. His voice was trembling, and for a moment she thought that he too must have seen.

Then she realized it wasn't that. The wretched youth was still pursuing his amorous fantasy. And of course he was scared stiff.

'Have you a torch – a match?' Judith was surprised to hear a voice that was entirely matter-of-fact, and to recognize it as her own.

'Well, yes – I have.' Thankful to do something non-committal, Pooh was fumbling in a pocket.

'Then shine it, please – just here.'

There was a long moment while he fumbled still. Then the beam shot out. 'On that?' she heard Pooh say. 'You're interested in that? There's a crowd of them in the art room. Didn't you notice?'

Judith stared at the recumbent figure. The river Nilus, perhaps. Anyway, a heathen divinity in dirty plaster – and there was the very hand her hand had clutched. 'Doesn't it look absurd?' she heard herself meaninglessly say – and even more meaninglessly add: 'I adore idiotic things like that. That's why I came exploring here. Lumber-rooms – don't you think? – are such heavenly fun?'

Pooh made an inarticulate noise. He must have laboriously trailed her here. And now he was trying to say something he conceived as relevant to the situation – perhaps that any lumber-room would be heavenly fun with Lady Appleby in it. But all the wretched lad managed was a mutter.

Judith dusted her knees and laughed. This time it was a genuine laugh and not a jolly one. Something had certainly died here and decomposed – and presumably it could only be a bird. But it was far from making the atmosphere insupportable. Nor did even Pooh do that. He was far too frightened to be other than rather touchingly absurd. And – of course – he could be useful.

'I'm so glad you have a torch,' Judith said. 'Do you know? Before I go home I'm quite, quite determined to peep at *all* this fascinating junk. Do you mind?'

Pooh didn't seem to mind. Like a man who knows his dream has faded, he obediently attended Judith as she poked about. She found, of course, nothing at all. But at least she had completed her assignment – and at no greater cost than that of a single moment of panic that it was already a little embarrassing to remember.

The thunder growled harmlessly in the middle distance. The storm had passed over Splaine Croft.

4

It was after dinner when Judith gave her husband a full account of her adventure. Although he was looking more careworn than she had known him for years, he professed to find a great deal of entertainment in it. She didn't take this too well.

'It was pretty futile, anyway,' she said. 'The place, after all, is a small estate. There's a lodge, and probably several cottages. Naturally, I couldn't get round to them. And your missing scientist might be lurking in any of them.'

'Yes – I suppose he might.' Appleby fiddled tiresomely with his empty coffee cup. 'Still, you got quite a lot of fun out of it.'

'I'm glad you feel I had a lovely time.' Judith looked at him wrathfully. 'What a strain it must be, having to find me lovely things to do, and lovely ladders to climb, and lovely puppies to be pestered by, and lovely smells to smell.'

Appleby continued to be amused. In fact he seemed genuinely to cheer up. 'As a matter of fact,' he said, 'you've brought back some very interesting information. Something I quite missed. It shows that two pairs of eyes are better than one. I'm not sure that it precisely fits in. But, of course, additional data can be all the better for that. One is compelled to some rearrangement. Do you know, I have a feeling I've got this whole thing wrong? A completely false picture? But I'm blessed if I can see just how.'

'I hadn't gathered you had a picture at all.' Judith hesitated. 'Incidentally, haven't you fixed up something pretty risky?'

'In persuading Miles Juniper to stand in for his brother? Well, yes – I suppose I have. There are circumstances in which it might become extremely awkward, however well I was backed up by the Minister, and so forth. But one takes these risks.'

'And hands them out too, surely? If this Howard Juniper is in some sort of danger – and also in some way immensely dangerous to others – wouldn't it be better to have an open and comprehensive search for him?'

'It's a thing just not easy to calculate.' Appleby got up and paced the room. 'As a matter of fact, I'm giving myself just twenty-four hours more. If I haven't found Howard Juniper by this time tomorrow, I pack off his brother to Splaine again, and have the disappearance announced. Meantime, I'm just hoping – if rather against hope – that the whole thing is a mare's nest, more or less. You remember Marchbanks?'

Judith nodded. 'Of course I remember Marchbanks.'

'Well, I think there may be a similar explanation here. And I've been having inquiries on appropriate lines made today. Some results have been negative. I'm waiting for the last batch now. There should be a telephone call from the Yard within the next half-hour.' Appleby paused before the Christopher Wood that hung above the fireplace. He might have been studying his favourite greys in the ballet-dancer's tights. 'Damn all top scientists!' he said with sudden vehemence.

Judith looked at him quickly. John didn't often resort even to the mildest imprecation. 'They do complicate life,' she said. 'But just why is this tiresome scientist so crucial? Or oughtn't I to know?'

'Everybody knows – although most people have no doubt forgotten again. The eminent Professor Juniper has been "featured", as they say, in all sorts of rags. Damn all newsprint too.' Appleby turned away from the little watercolour and faced his wife. 'If you wanted to exterminate the inhabitants of these islands – or, for that matter, of much larger areas of the earth's surface – this Juniper would be the chap to hire. And, as soon as he's known to be missing, that's what the banner headlines will point out.'

'There oughtn't to be such a man.' Judith was suddenly grave. 'He oughtn't to have lent his abilities to such madness. He oughtn't to have been required to.'

'That's pretty obvious, I'd suppose.' Appleby was restless again. 'It's what his brother thinks. It's what Clandon probably thinks. It's what we think, and what every sane man thinks. But there it is. It's just part of the rat race… Why doesn't that telephone call come through?'

They went up to the drawing-room. In London, too, there had been a storm, but now the windows were open on the warm summer night. Big Ben struck the hour close by, and the heavy sound tumbled into the room like a physical thing. Judith got out some brandy, but neither of them poured any. They sat down to wait.

'Mid-August,' she said vaguely. 'I suppose we're the only people left in London.'

'The only people left in London?' He took up the words oddly. 'We might be, I suppose. Any two people might be, if one or another thing happened.'

'Oh – that!' She shook her head. 'I've always been impatient – haven't I? – with people scared about our all going up together. I've felt it to be only a kind of phobia. But perhaps that's irresponsible.'

'Perhaps it is.'

'Do you think there are people who would welcome it – nobody left in London? Is there that sort of pathologically destructive mind?'

'It's a question one sometimes hears asked.' Appleby shook his head. 'I suppose there may be.'

'There was Richard Jefferies. You remember *After London*? He thought the city had killed him, and was killing all England as well. So he wrote a fantasy in which he killed London. It was a sort of revenge.'

'And, of course, there's Macaulay's New Zealander.' Appleby, restless still, did his best to keep up this desultory talk. 'In the midst of a vast solitude, taking his stand on a broken arch of London Bridge to sketch the ruins of St Paul's. Something like that.'

'Yes.'

The clock ticked. 'As I say,' Appleby said, 'there's a hope that the whole thing's a baseless scare.'

'And just what is the position, if it isn't? I mean, is Professor Juniper potentially so lethal just because of what he keeps under his hat, or has he – '

'Possibly both.' Appleby didn't wait for Judith to finish. 'There's certainly what he *knows*, just as there's what the top flight nuclear people *know*. And there may be what he *has* – more or less literally in his pocket. A culture – or whatever they call it – of almost inconceivable virulence. Clandon says he can't be sure. He hopes and thinks not. But he can't be sure.'

'And there's been no trace of him – not even a trail picked up for a bit and then lost?'

'Absolutely not. He walked out – without a word, it seems, and without so much as a briefcase. The earth might have swallowed him.'

'Or the waters.'

'Quite so. And the waters wouldn't be too bad. Sooner or later, they'd render up something, and we'd know where we were.'

Judith was silent for a moment. She had the resource of darning socks. 'There must be lots of ways,' she said presently, 'in which a clever man can commit suicide without leaving a trace of himself.'

'Lord, yes. But why should Juniper do that? In his circumstances, it would be a most devilish trick. What motive would he have?'

'That's easy, surely. Suppose it has all got him down far more than anybody suspected. Suppose he has suffered indescribably in his conscience simply because of working in that field. He can't face it, and he takes his own life. But he does it in a way that gets him a little of his own back on authority and government and so on. He's not prompted to go so far as scattering his microbes or whatever they are. But he does fix things so that a good many of you don't sleep too well.'

Appleby shook his head. 'Yes – but he doesn't seem to have been quite that sort of person. Nervous and erratic, perhaps – but not even incipiently malignant. I've had all this out with medical chaps thoroughly reliable in their field. They incline to the view – naturally they won't be dogmatic – that a theory like yours posits a personality

71

change that doesn't come on a man suddenly and without his associates being aware that something's going wrong. And there's not the slightest record that Howard Juniper has had what could reasonably be called a psychiatric history.'

'But isn't it something that a man can have on the quiet? Not everybody revels in broadcasting their experiences on a psycho-analyst's couch. Although certainly some do.'

'Yes – it has to be admitted as a possibility. But it's not a substantial one during recent years. Farther back, it's a different matter… Ah, there's the doorbell. Cudworth must have decided to come round. Too complicated for the telephone. I'm not sure that isn't hopeful.'

Superintendent Cudworth was a large man, and he seemed to occupy a disproportionate space in the cubbyhole that served Appleby as a study in the small Westminster house. He was in uniform and his silver-braided cap lay on the desk; he himself stood by the window turning over a sheaf of notes. From the deliberation with which he continued to do this for a moment, Appleby knew that he was excited. 'Out with it, Cudworth,' he said.

'You got on a winner, sir. Birds it is. Or at least it looks uncommonly like it. Bit of a relief, you might say, if it really turns out that way.'

'Oh, quite.' Appleby was perfectly capable of matching Cudworth's power of understatement. 'Just how has it worked out?'

'Well, sir, it didn't seem to me to be too promising, as you know. I remembered your fellow who was found trout fishing, all right. Well, they say that's the contemplative man's recreation. You don't normally go off to it in a crowd. And it seemed to me that the same would apply *a fortiori* to birdwatching. A thoroughly solitary employment. One tucks oneself away in some out-of-the-way country pub, and one's only companion is one's binoculars. And I'm sure, in fact, that most birdwatching is done that way. On the other hand, there does turn out to be a certain amount of organization.'

Appleby nodded. 'I knew there was. My wife subscribes to an affair somewhere on the Severn.'

'The Wildfowl Trust, that would be. An important concern in the field of ornithological science. And there are one or two others. They even have hostels for members, and so on. A fellow at Burlington House briefed me about the whole thing in no time, and we've had the local police making inquiries. They all drew blank. But that, I'm glad to say, was only Phase One.'

'Phase Two,' Appleby said.

'Phase Two, sir, has been concerned not with public bodies but with private individuals. And it has been a bigger job. Particularly, of course, since it was necessary to take in Scotland, Ireland, and Wales. There are a good many owners of large estates who maintain sanctuaries, reserves, and what have you – and who are perfectly willing to admit, and even entertain, well-accredited students of the thing. All as you might imagine.'

'Quite,' Appleby said.

'Professor Juniper, if he really had this interest in birds, would know about all that pretty well. I mean that a fellow with a highly trained mind, and so forth, would naturally get a grip of the entire set-up. And he'd have the entrée, as they say. Get in, I mean, wherever he wanted to.'

'Obviously,' Appleby said.

'Well, no – that's just the point. There are one or two landowners with the relevant interests who don't welcome anybody. *Keep Out. This Means You.* That sort.'

'In which case, no doubt, the enthusiast lurks on the fringes and observes what he can?'

'Just that. And the most notorious of them is the Earl of Ailsworth. Would you have heard of him?'

Appleby shook his head. 'I can't say I have.'

'No more you would have. A backwoodsman, as they say. Not much on view over *there*' – and at this Superintendent Cudworth jerked a thumb in what was presumably meant to be the direction of the House of Lords – 'but well known if you happen to be interested in birds. Particularly on account of the Tibetan Donkey Duck.'

'The Tibetan Donkey Duck? There can't be such a creature. The name's absurd.'

'Well, sir, the point is there *nearly* wasn't such a creature. The species had almost died out. But Lord Ailsworth led an expedition in search of them, and actually found a couple – '

'In Tibet?'

'Certainly in Tibet. And he brought them home and has managed to breed from them. But he keeps them, it seems, very much to himself.'

Appleby smiled. 'One can understand a somewhat proprietary attitude in the circumstances. And now, let us have it, Cudworth. You've established a link between this Lord Ailsworth, and the missing man?'

'Well, sir – yes and no. Ailsworth is a small market town, and I got on to the police there straight away. They were uncooperative, I'm sorry to say. Scared of bothering the local bigwig.'

'Common enough.'

'There's no doubt of that. So I wasted no time on them, but contacted their Chief Constable. Name of Colonel Pickering. Well, that seemed all right. Probably accustomed to drinking his lordship's port, and all the rest of it. And he sounded a very nice fellow. Told me he'd do what he could, but that I'd landed him with a stiff assignment. Lord Ailsworth's quite mad, he said. Can think of nothing but the Donkey Ducks.' Cudworth broke off. 'Did you say the name troubled you? A matter of markings on the breast, it seems. Like the head of a donkey.'

'Bother the bird and its idiotic name. What came of all this?'

'A thoroughly negative report, as far as Colonel Pickering was concerned. He had managed to see Lord Ailsworth, but came away with nothing but a flea in his ear. Lord Ailsworth had never heard of anybody called Juniper. And anybody who came disturbing his birds would be shot. Just that.'

'Forthright.'

'Forthright, as you say. But I had a feeling that this Ailsworth line should be followed up. Lord Ailsworth and his Donkey Ducks suggest a sort of challenge, wouldn't you say? And I remembered Professor Juniper's reputation for queer exploits as a young man. There was food for thought in it.'

'There certainly was.' Appleby, for the first time, nodded in brisk approval. 'Next?'

'I thought of precisely the situation you mentioned, sir. The baffled enthusiast lurking in the nearest pub. And I sent a sergeant down by car straight away. There are a couple of hotels in Ailsworth itself, where he drew quite blank. But in an isolated hamlet called Nether Ailsworth, on the edge of Lord Ailsworth's park, it was another matter. The people in the pub recognized a photograph of Professor Juniper at once. He'd stayed there for a couple of nights about six weeks ago. I've checked on the dates since. Juniper ought to have been in Edinburgh. He'd given it out that he was making a dash there to contact a biologist over on a short visit from Denmark. Of course it was nobody's business to corroborate such an announcement by the boss of the Research Station.'

Appleby took a deep breath. 'It's a trail,' he said.

'Yes, sir – or something getting on that way. I must say that the first thing I thought of was the possibility of confusion with Professor Juniper's brother. *He* might be keen on birds too. But the sergeant had covered the whole business. There had been no concealment. Howard Juniper's name, in Howard Juniper's writing, was there in the pub register. And even the Research Station as his address.'

'But after that – nothing?'

'Nothing. If our man has been back to Ailsworth, it hasn't been to that pub.'

5

Appleby drove himself down to Ailsworth very early in the morning. Short of a Cabinet Minister, he was the only appropriate person for the job. For if Howard Juniper was really going to be run to earth while happily trespassing on the Earl of Ailsworth's bird sanctuary, he would decidedly have to be put on the carpet. The metaphors were a bit mixed, Appleby thought, but they did cover the facts of the situation. Juniper was a very big man, and it wouldn't do to preach to him or adopt a high moral tone. What such a man would be most likely to take in good part would be words spoken more in anger than in sorrow. And Appleby didn't think he would find it difficult to be very genuinely angry. He would indeed be far less angry than relieved. But he needn't show that.

Of course he could only take Howard Juniper that way if the chap was reasonably sane. If Juniper's bolt had been the consequence of a bad breakdown, Appleby's responsibility would obviously be confined to calling in the doctors. But supposing – what was much more probable – that Juniper wasn't very definitely one thing or the other? What might become important then, surely, would be some ability to enter into his point of view.

Appleby wished he knew more about birds. If it had been proper to bring Judith – and why hadn't he, since it had certainly not been particularly proper to send her to Splaine Croft? – she would have handled that side of the situation adequately. As a boy he had collected birds' eggs – which was now just one more of the things you couldn't legally do. Who would be a policeman – he asked himself irrelevantly, as he ran along the Suffolk coast – in an age in which

76

small boys must be brought before magistrates and lectured on the wickedness of rifling hedgerows?

This birdwatching business clearly happened at a number of levels. At the lowest, the small boys, warned off their bird-nesting, made lists of birds seen, accompanied by appropriate smudgy drawings. That was rather like collecting the numbers of railway engines – although it was fair to admit that, humanly, it was rather more promising. Then there were all sorts of serious adults, with schoolmasters – one would say at a guess – heading the list. Miles Juniper, in fact, rather than Howard. But, beyond that, there were no doubt people of highly intellectual habit who found in crawling about with binoculars some sort of release from obsessional labour in the field of science. Howard Juniper came in there.

But why birds? What did the little blighters do that was so compelling? Appleby, although he had in fact some claim to be a countryman, asked himself this question in a conscientiously townee way. Clearly the answer was that birds have a life of their own which, although over large areas irrational and perplexing, isn't quite so irrational and perplexing as the life that human beings have been contriving for themselves of late. Work hard on birds, and you may here and there make some sense of them. This scarcely holds of *homo sapiens*.

The road swung west to skirt an estuary. He stopped the car and studied his map. Yes, there it was – on the other side of this broad empty stretch of water. Marshland, and then water meadow with pollarded trees marking the lines of ditches. Beyond that, on slightly higher ground, some areas of timber. Just visible behind the largest of these, a pediment and a cluster of chimneys. Ailsworth Court.

He must go some miles west still to the first bridge across the estuary. On this side he skirted lazily lapping water which was a lovely summer blue. But on the other side were great stretches of reed which it would be hard to push a boat through. Straight opposite where he had stopped the car, he could see a high wire fence running down to the water and some way into it. Getting out his binoculars – which might be useful for spotting more than birds – and scanning the farther shore to the west of this, he could distinguish, more than a couple of miles away, the last hundred yards of a similar fence. They were fences of the formidable sort that incline outwards at the top at an angle of forty-five degrees. It was evident that Lord Ailsworth took the protecting of his birds very seriously.

Appleby drove on. Nether Ailsworth proved to be a dull little place, and its pub, the Bell, looked primitive and uninviting. It was inconceivable that Howard Juniper could ever have chosen it on its merits for a quiet holiday. Lord Ailsworth's sanctuary emerged quite clearly as the only reason why he could have wished to come near the place. Appleby decided, provisionally, to come back to the Bell for lunch; it would certainly not be much of a meal, but he might pick up further information. At the moment, he would go straight on to Ailsworth Court, and see whether he had better luck with its owner than Colonel Pickering had reported.

Again he drove on – this time skirting a high stone wall uncompromisingly crowned with broken glass. The map showed only one drive of any consequence as leading to the mansion, and within a couple of minutes he had reached it. Flanked by symmetrical lodges which could never much have consulted the convenience of their occupants, and hung on massive stone pilasters crowned with prancing griffins, wrought-iron gates of great elaboration were inhospitably closed against the world. Appleby drew up with his bonnet facing them and sounded his horn. Childe Rowland, he said to himself, to the dark tower comes.

Nothing happened. The earl's retainers – hurrying or loitering, scowling or bobbing, aged or juvenile – were not in evidence. Appleby got out and prospected. The lodges were deserted, and their windows were boarded up. The iron gates, which were rusty and uncared for, were secured by an equally rusty chain and padlock. Appleby peered through them and up the drive. It was, in fact, a long elm avenue, and in a state of utter neglect. It was deep in leaf mould, with here and there tussocks of bleached summer grass. A hundred yards or so ahead, a great elm had come down in a way that seemed to make wheeled traffic impossible. Ailsworth Court itself was invisible.

It was a set-up that took Appleby entirely by surprise. He hadn't been able to find out a great deal about Lord Ailsworth, but at least he had sufficient information to be certain that he was far from belonging to the more picturesquely indigent of our ancient nobility. The Ailsworths weren't at all ancient – except indeed as prosperous citizens, a station they had owned in the time of the first Elizabeth. The present Lord Ailsworth was the third earl. And it was the first earl who had made the family breweries the biggest concern of their kind in England. Lack of money certainly wasn't the occasion of the forlorn face that the place chose to present to the world. And that left only one explanation. Lord Ailsworth must be a person of pronounced eccentricity. Appleby looked forward to meeting him.

This, however, didn't seem too easy to achieve. There must, of course, be some other entrance to Ailsworth Court. Even if its owner were a recluse, a certain amount of coming and going was inevitable. Somewhere there must be at least a cart-track. And he was bound to find it if he nosed around. Or he could simply go back to the Bell and inquire.

But Appleby's glance, as he made these reflections, was on the rusty iron gates. He found himself considering footholds and estimating distances. And he thought of Judith, storming that loft at Splaine Croft. Need he himself take up a more elderly attitude? He looked up and down the road. It was entirely deserted. He peered through the gates at the neglected avenue. It seemed entirely deserted too. And there was no physical impediment to his making the climb. He was as fit now as he had been twenty years ago. No, the only impediment was a matter of decorum and dignity. Top people don't go over the top; they expect to be ceremoniously ushered through… Appleby began to climb.

It wasn't easy. In fact he had seriously underestimated the task. The gates, after all, although elaborately got up with volutes and scrolls, had been designed in the first place just as *gates*. And they were doing their job tolerably well. They had already exacted from Appleby the forfeit of rather a large rent in a cherished piece of Lovat

MICHAEL INNES

tweed. Still, he had got to the top. But the main difficulty was to get down again.

Above the gates was more ironwork, pyramidal in structure, and supporting a large shield on which armorial bearings had at one time been enamelled. The Ailsworth hogsheads and firkins and tankards, he thought to himself with a certain ill temper. He was astride this final pompous if decayed affair, and conscious of the distinct possibility of a further laceration in the seat of his trousers, when he saw that he was being observed.

A young woman had appeared in the avenue. She was dressed in breeches and leggings, and she carried a pail. She was looking up at him with startled – almost, he thought, with haunted – eyes. But when she spoke, it was in a manner that was entirely self-possessed.

'Are you coming, or going?' the young woman asked.

Gowing is always Cumming, and Cumming is always Gowing. For a moment it was only this ancient and idiotic joke that Appleby could think of by way of reply. And of course it would be rather too inconsequent to be satisfactory. So he just looked at the young woman, and the young woman looked at him. After all, he *was* elderly, or at least getting on that way. And dignity and decorum sat as naturally on him as did the excellent old Lovat. His hair was grey at the temples. He looked most natural in a black soft hat – and even tolerably natural in a bowler and a beard, like the late notable Mr Clwyd. If he were twenty-two, this would be fine. He would grin cheerfully at the young woman from his elevated perch, and probably all would be well. As it was, his was at the moment a demonstrably false position.

'Coming,' Appleby said.

'Then why don't you move *laterally*?' the young woman said. 'Like a crab. You can reach one of the stone pillars that way. And come down by the rustications.'

Appleby saw that this was a good suggestion. He saw, too, that the young woman was not a milkmaid, or person of similar rustic quality. Far from it. You have Lady Margaret Hall – he said to himself – written all over you. And probably you're cracked on birds. Aloud, he said: 'Thank you. I'll take your advice. And then perhaps we can talk.'

The young woman made no reply to this. She watched his descent impassively. 'You've ripped your jacket,' she said, when he had come to earth. 'And,' she added with quiet satisfaction, 'your trousers too.' Her glance went to the leather binocular case slung over his shoulder. 'I suppose,' she asked coldly, 'it's the Perry River White-fronted Goose?'

'No,' Appleby said. 'It's not that. Definitely not that.' He was still feeling rather foolish.

'Then it must be the Fulvous Whistling Duck.' The young woman announced this with quiet certainty. 'Those are the two there has been talk about lately.'

'Not that either. I'm not interested in birds.'

'Are you not, indeed?' The girl's voice hardened. She was abruptly demoting Appleby from the status of impertinent enthusiast to that of plain thief, intent on walking out with a Fulvous Whistling Duck in his pocket. 'I think you'd better explain that to the police.'

'I *am* the police.'

'Nonsense. You're a gentleman.' The girl flushed slightly, as if conscious of having unwarily said something idiotic. 'I mean you're a genteel crook. It's written all over you.'

'Don't be absurd, child. It's nothing of that sort.' Appleby felt that only a certain heavy paternal quality could quite make up for the memory of him perched grotesquely at the apex of Lord Ailsworth's gates. 'My name is John Appleby. I'll find you a card.'

'My name is Jean Howe. And I don't in the least want to see your card. I expect you have dozens of them.'

'Then I won't bother you with it.' Appleby looked at Miss Howe with some amusement. 'Why do you keep your garden gate padlocked in that curmudgeonly way?'

'Our garden gate?' She looked at him suspiciously, as if conscious of being made fun of. 'I suppose we're entitled to such privacy as we choose? After all, it's our own land.'

'But don't you think it should all be nationalized, and so forth?'

Appleby realized that this random and absurd question was a great success. It involved the young woman, whose views were conscientiously advanced, in difficulty that was for the moment insuperable. However, she came back not badly. 'Did you climb in,' she asked, 'and ruin that very decent suit, just for the luxury of debating socialism with the first person who detected you?'

'I climbed in to see Lord Ailsworth. I think you are a relation of his? I remember the family name.'

'I'm his granddaughter.' As she took in more of the intruder, the young woman was growing visibly perplexed. 'I don't understand what you mean,' she said, 'by calling yourself the police. But I know that Colonel Pickering came to see my grandfather yesterday.'

'Quite so. And he doesn't seem to have been terribly well received. Lord Ailsworth talked about shooting anybody who came hanging round the place. Is he always like that?'

Jean Howe looked worried. 'Not a bit. He is very shy and retired, and so he has got himself a reputation for being odd. But he is usually the kindest and gentlest of men. Just sometimes he has queer fits of anger, which get exaggerated by gossip.' The girl gave Appleby a quick apprehensive glance. 'You haven't come because people have been saying he is really mad?'

'Quite definitely not. I come from Scotland Yard, not Harley Street.'

Jean looked relieved. 'You see, these sudden flares of temper or intense feeling are just something in the family. I get them myself.'

'Really?' Appleby smiled at her. 'What about?'

'Oh – just the way of the world in general.' Jean spoke quickly, as if this was something she was not prepared to enter upon.

Appleby changed the subject. 'You live here?' he asked.

'Well, I used to – off and on. I like the birds. For the last three years, I've been here only now and then during university vacations. This time, I've been here only a few days. But I expect I shall stop.' Jean hesitated. 'I expect I shall *have* to stop.'

They had turned and were walking down the avenue. Appleby was thinking cautiously that he had begun to establish a relation of confidence with this young woman. Which was lucky – because she didn't strike him as an easy girl. And the circumstances of their first introduction to each other hadn't been exactly propitious.

'You feel you may have to stay here?' he prompted gently. 'Do you mean that you find your grandfather needing rather more looking after than formerly?'

'The whole set-up needs that. You see, he is quite obsessed with the birds.'

'At an effective scientific level?'

'Oh, dear me – yes. Even the mere collection of pinioned birds here is very important. But his work on the snaring and ringing, and at receiving reports from all over the world and compiling his census, has very high standing among ornithologists. He lives for it. Although perhaps it would be fair to say that he lives more and more for the birds and less and less for the ornithologists.'

'And the estate, and so forth: does he at all live for that?'

Jean made a gesture at the decay around them. 'You can see he doesn't. Nor for the house, either – although it has been rather a place in its time. The domestic situation there is difficult. Perhaps sketchy would be the word. That's the chief reason why I think I'll have to stay about. My father was the only son, you see. And he was killed in the war. My mother died when I was a baby. And most of our relations keep well away. They've no interest, because it's all fixed up that a direct heir succeeds, even if a female. That will be me.'

'You mean,' Appleby asked, 'that you will be a peeress in your own right?'

'I don't know. I've never inquired.' Jean seemed genuinely indifferent. 'But I shall have the birds.'

They turned a corner of the drive, and Ailsworth Court was before them. James Gibbs, Appleby said to himself – being stronger on buildings than on birds. There was a massive central block, linked by quadrant corridors to two service wings. The domestic situation could very readily become difficult, one supposed, where the architect had designed that your dinner should come to you along a hundred yards of curved passageway. But at least it was extremely grand – and as each of the service wings had an identical lantern with an identical clock, you would always know when to hurry home to meet the advancing feast. If – that was to say – the clocks were in working order, which they didn't look to have been for a long time. The whole of Ailsworth Court, in fact, looked uncared for, unlived in, dilapidated, and almost ready to tumble down.

Lord Ailsworth's granddaughter had come to a halt. Approaching the house thus in company with a stranger, she seemed to find it a little daunting. 'You can see,' she said, 'that we've seen better days.'

'But your grandfather is wealthy?'

'Of course. He has far more money than is decent. It's not that. It's just that he doesn't any longer much care for people, and he won't have them about. No guests. And no masons or carpenters or painters either.'

'That's fairly evident. But the birds seem to like it.'

This was fairly evident too. The whole façade, together with a row of colossal statues perched above the cornice, was white with their droppings.

'It is rather startling, I'm afraid. Particularly inside.'

'Inside!' Appleby was astonished. 'You don't mean that the birds are – well, in residence?'

'They have infiltrated rather, of recent years. My grandfather doesn't see why the whole place should be empty. There are wild duck in the attics. It sounds like Ibsen, doesn't it?' Jean smiled faintly. 'And, of course, the Donkey Ducks are in the drawing-room. You must have heard about them.'

'The ones that Lord Ailsworth rescued from extinction?' Appleby nodded. 'I suppose it's natural that they should be given the place of honour in the household. But are *all* the birds parlour boarders? Don't some live out?'

Jean laughed. 'The great majority live out. The pens are on the other side of the house, running down to the breeding ground and the decoy pool and the river. Would you like to see them before we hunt out my grandfather?' She looked at her watch. 'I don't think he'll be about yet, as a matter of fact. And it will give you something to talk about.' She paused. 'If, that's to say, he's at all disposed to talk to you.'

'If it's not taking up too much of your time,' Appleby said.

He suspected that Miss Howe's offer was a matter neither of pure benevolence nor of simple pride in what she had to display. She wanted to know more about the stranger and his business before she admitted him to her grandfather's presence. And that, in the circumstances, seemed fair enough. What Appleby had to decide was how much he was going to confide in her.

'We'll go this way.' Jean, who had disposed of her bucket, led the way down a path which made a wide detour of the house. 'I'll simply show you some of the pens, and then take you up the nearer observation tower and explain how the decoy pool works.'

'Thank you. I'll be most interested.'

'But I think you said you're *not* interested in birds?' Jean was slightly mocking. 'When people are frank about that, I usually show them just the Trumpeter Swans and the Cackling Geese.'

'Don't all geese cackle? I seem to remember it's what they did on the Capitol, when they gave the alarm and saved Rome from somebody or other.'

Jean turned and faced him. 'Could you possibly,' she said, 'cut the cackle? And tell me what all this is about?'

'It's about a very eminent scientist who has disappeared.' Appleby had come to a decision about this young woman. 'His name is Juniper.'

'Juniper?' Jean frowned. 'It's an uncommon name. But it seems to ring some bell.'

'Very probably. He's been in the news from time to time.'

'But the bell seems fairly recent.' Jean shook her head. 'But what has his disappearance got to do with us down here?'

'We've been unearthing his various interests. And one of them has proved to be birdwatching. We've been following that up. And we've discovered that he was in Nether Ailsworth only a few weeks before he vanished. He was clearly interested in your set-up here.'

'I don't see that it would have been of much use his coming down. My grandfather has been frightfully anti-visitor of late. As those gates will have made you realize.'

'Quite so,' Appleby said – and unconsciously fingered the tear in his jacket. 'Shall you get in a row for showing me round?'

'I hope not. And this was what Colonel Pickering came about yesterday? He hoped to learn if my grandfather knew anything about this man Juniper?'

'Just that. And Lord Ailsworth said he's never heard of him.'

'Then why should you come today?' Jean asked this rather stiffly. 'My grandfather may be eccentric – and even rude at times. But he's not a liar.'

'My dear young woman, I don't question for a moment that Lord Ailsworth is a man of the strictest honour. But this fellow Juniper – Howard Juniper – happens to have an eccentric strain in him too, or at least he cultivated one as a younger man. Although he came down here openly some weeks ago, he may have come down later masquerading as somebody quite different. Your grandfather may have been subjected to a deception. That's why I want some talk with him.'

Jean had halted before what appeared to be the first of the pens. 'Just the Common Shoveler,' she said. 'But attractive, don't you think?'

Appleby examined the creature with civil interest. 'I like the glaucous blue,' he pronounced.

'On the lesser wing coverts? Yes, indeed. And just look at the speculum.'

Appleby did his best to look as if he were looking at the speculum. 'Remarkable,' he said.

'You don't know what I'm talking about. We'll move on. You'd better see the Ruddy Shelduck.'

'Yes, I should enjoy that.'

'And – by the way – I think I'd like to look at that card, after all.'

Appleby produced his pocketbook and handed her a card. 'That's very sensible of you,' he said with a return to his paternal manner.

She glanced at it and walked for a moment in silence. Then she looked at him with fresh curiosity. 'Do you generally do your own chasing after missing persons, Sir John?'

'No, hardly ever. I lead, nowadays, a shockingly inactive life. But I've been rather chivvied into this.'

'And who is in a position to chivvy you?'

'Oh, several people. The Prime Minister, among others.'

'You're not having me on?'

'No, I'm not. I ought to say, by the way, that I hope simply to find this infuriating Howard Juniper and lead him quietly home. Without any publicity at all. So my story to you is confidential.'

'I'm not likely to ring up the local paper.' Jean said this with a sharp contempt no doubt appropriate in the granddaughter of an earl. 'And I'm prepared to accept your missing scientist as somebody terribly important. What's his line?'

'He's a bacteriologist.'

'It sounds as if he was quite a useful sort of person. But do Prime Ministers often bother their heads about missing bacteriologists, however eminent?'

'Not at all often.'

Jean came to a dead halt. 'And what did you say his name was?'

'Juniper. Howard Juniper. You seem a bit surprised.'

'Do I? I was just remembering something. Now we'll do the observation tower.'

6

The observation tower was unimpressive. It was like a very large packing case on stilts, and a ladder led up to it. Head high, there was a narrow unglazed aperture all round. A draughty place in winter, Appleby thought.

Although not high, it yet commanded, over this flat country and the broad stretches of water beyond, a remarkable view. It was an uncommonly deserted tract of country, Appleby thought, and admirably adapted to be some sort of nature reserve. Just visible on the other side of the estuary was the road along which he had himself driven. But there seemed to be not so much as a cottage on it, and only far to the east a smudge of black smoke gave some suggestion of industrial activity. And on this side, apart from the chimneys of Ailsworth Court just visible about a quarter of a mile to the north, there was nothing except a few low sheds and – far out towards the river – a second observation tower. What at first caught one's attention, however, lay quite near at hand. It was a large pool, connected by a broad channel with the estuary, and having four arms which gave it the shape of a conventional star. Each arm led into a sort of openwork tunnel, apparently constructed of wire netting, which curved gently and grew narrower until it ended as a straitened cul-de-sac. It was rather as if four skeletal cornucopias had been thrown down at the corners of the pool – except, presumably, that they were designed not to pour anything out but to entice something in.

Appleby studied the arrangement with real interest. 'I can see,' he said, 'that waterfowl will settle on the pool. But what persuades them to swim up these sinister-looking tunnels?'

Jean Howe laughed. 'I don't think you'd guess the answer at all easily. It's a dog.'

'A dog? You mean it swims after them?'

'Not at all. You see the wattle screens flanking the tunnels, as you call them? And the gaps in them, here and there? The dog is simply trained to show himself successively at the different gaps, and always working up towards the neck of the trap. He doesn't chase the fowl. The fowl chase him. Nobody knows why. But they do. Then one of the men – my grandfather has three or four – appears at the mouth of the trap in a dinghy and drives them forward.'

'How very odd.' Appleby was genuinely impressed. 'And then the birds are caught and ringed and so forth?'

'Just that. And, next year, we shall hear of them turning up in Hawaii or Siberia or wherever. The study of migration, you know, is absolutely fascinating. It's absolutely absorbing. I can't tell you.'

'I don't doubt it.' Appleby was aware that Jean had spoken with a sudden intensity which suggested that her grandfather's master passion was getting a firm grip on her too. 'Am I right,' he added, 'in thinking that the fascination comes in part from the whole purpose and mechanism of the thing being largely inexplicable?'

'Well, one can occasionally see why birds go to and fro within their range. It's a simple matter of climate and food. But not always. One has to suppose that they are still doing something that ceased to have any point ages and ages ago. And, you know, it isn't only birds. Butterflies can be even more mysterious. Painted Ladies come out of their chrysalises in the Sudan and move straight north in hordes. They may end up in the Arctic Circle, which doesn't seem sensible at all. There are other kinds that fly straight out to sea until they fall and drown. But the birds, of course, are the long-distance champions. The North American Golden Plover thinks nothing of 2,000 miles non-stop over the Atlantic. And there's really no explanation of why it makes the effort. But the *how* of the thing is more mysterious still.

The first broods of young swallows, you know, leave England before their parents – and make their own way to the tribe's prescriptive winter quarters in South Africa. And in the following spring they may return to the very barn in which they were hatched. For countless centuries every one of the little creatures has been born with its own radar and so forth ready built-in. It's impressive. But if one wants really to scare oneself, one has to turn from the butterflies and birds to some of the small mammals. Do you know about the Lemmings?'

Appleby considered. 'Don't they,' he asked cautiously, 'behave with some degree of folly?'

'Their behaviour isn't technically migration, because they never come back. It's irruption. Every now and then their numbers rocket up – nobody knows why. So food grows scarce, and they get on the move. That's sensible enough. But their one idea is to move on a dead straight line. There may be millions and millions of them, obsessed with this necessity to turn themselves into a vast crawling Roman road. They turn aside for nothing at all. When they get to the sea – as they're bound to do in the end – they don't turn aside for that either. They swim straight out into it till they drown.'

'It's disturbing,' Appleby said.

'Just that. You've found a splendid word for it.' Jean spoke ironically, but her voice was tense with the excitement of some inward vision. 'Ages and ages ago, this forward-march business must have had some positive biological value. It was what, if you were a Lemming, in certain circumstances got you through. So Lemmings, when they get rattled, do just the same thing today – and will go on doing it, one supposes, as long as any Lemmings are. Don't you think, Sir John, viewing human behaviour as a whole, that it's the Lemming and not the Lemur or the Chimpanzee that has most claim to cousinship with us?'

She hadn't spoken for effect; it wasn't like a clever point in an undergraduate debate. A certain impulse towards sombre philosophical reflection was perhaps constitutional among the Howes. And Appleby had a sudden and alarming picture of this intermittently brooding and intense girl forty years on – if somebody didn't come along and rescue her from Ailsworth and its birds. She would be as cranky as her grandfather was said to be now. And this would be a great shame. An attractive as well as an intelligent girl.

There was a flight of wild duck in the air, and across the pool some swans were majestically gliding. But what one was chiefly aware of was silence and the empty sky.

'You spend quite a lot of time here, when you're at Ailsworth?' Appleby asked.

'Quite a lot. It depends on the season.' Jean caught his glance and laughed. 'You're thinking it's all rather bleak and lonesome? It isn't, if you understand what's happening. I think I could spend my life very happily here – if I didn't have an idea that it would be a kind of running away. To get like my grandfather – frankly preferring feathered to unfeathered bipeds – is rather throwing up the sponge, don't you think?'

'Well, yes.' Appleby smiled. 'That's to say, I think it may be all right in an elderly eccentric. Your grandfather no doubt does good work on the feathered tribes, whereas he might be a mere nuisance in the House of Lords. But I'd deprecate it in a young woman.' He took a last look out over the empty landscape, and turned to descend the ladder. 'But I'm not sure, myself, that I'd find your birds the best way of escaping from a contemplation of the human condition. Certainly not the migrating ones. They get together in mobs for the purpose of performing prodigious but senseless acts. That's precisely the state of the case in our own world. Lemmings, birds, or men: there's really nothing to choose between them.'

Jean laughed. 'You'd better not make that a line of talk with my grandfather. Why, there he is! He's been to the other tower. He keeps the big maps there, and allows nobody near the place. He likes to make a secret of them until he really has something to communicate.'

Appleby, who had been about to scramble down the ladder, turned back and looked out. At the moment, Lord Ailsworth was a barely distinguishable figure. One might have taken him for one of his own ducks – the more so as he appeared to be advancing mysteriously on the surface of a patch of water. 'Is he wading?' Appleby asked.

'No. There are several little causeys, although it's hard to see them. Can you make out what's following him? Use your field glasses, if you can't.'

Appleby got out his binoculars. What was following Lord Ailsworth was really ducks: a sedately waddling line of them. Lord Ailsworth himself turned out to be a long-legged man with a stoop – less a duck, after all, than a heron. As Appleby watched, he stopped, turned, and appeared to address the creatures that were following him. Then he rummaged in a basket which he carried over his arm, scattered something, and walked on.

'We'll go and meet him,' Jean said. And she added, with a touch of mockery, 'It will be fun seeing what you make of each other.'

'I'm sure it will. But please remember that my actual business isn't at all funny.' Appleby was serious. 'I'd like to think I can rely on you to back me up.'

'I'll do what I can, of course, Sir John.'

'Thank you. By the way, what are the big maps?'

'Maps of the world. There's a storey in the other tower which has its walls lined with them. When a bird that has been ringed here is reported as caught and recorded in another country, the place is marked with a coloured bead. You know the sort of war film in which people keep track of air raids, and so on, on enormous charts? It always reminds me of that.'

'With your grandfather as a sort of Air Marshal, sending his winged squadrons hither and thither about the globe? It's another queer parallel between birds and men.'

'Except that men carry bombs, and birds carry nothing but their own identification papers.'

They had reached the ground, and Lord Ailsworth was no longer visible. But Jean set a brisk pace in the direction from which he would come. For a couple of minutes they walked in silence. There were more pens, but Appleby didn't much attend to them. At least, he was telling himself, one couldn't find more appropriate territory upon which to conduct a wild-goose chase. He had sent Judith on one yesterday, and he had himself embarked on one today. That, at least, was the sober probability of the matter. Unless, of course –

He turned suddenly to Jean. 'Out there where your grandfather is now,' he said. 'Is it dangerous? Would it be risky for someone who didn't know the place to go prowling over all that marshland?'

'I'd scarcely suppose so. There can't be any deep water to drown in, or the sort of mud in which one can sink and leave nothing but bubbles. And it's late in the season for my grandfather to feel he must take a shot at anybody trespassing on the breeding grounds.'

'Would he really do that? It sounds a little feudal and high-handed.'

'Of course not. There have been incidents in which he has raved at intruders in a most alarming way. But I've never known him *do* anything as a result of that sort of brainstorm... Now then, here he is.'

They had walked down a long path past a line of pens sheltering a variety of exotic fowl. Lord Ailsworth had paused beside the last of these, set down his basket, and stooped over a bird. Now he straightened up. He was older than Appleby had supposed – a worn and haggard man, with craggy features, and long and untidy white hair. His expression was gentle and withdrawn – a fact which made the more startling the extraordinary brightness of his deep blue eyes.

'The Andean Crested Duck,' he said. 'Something not quite right about him, I'm afraid. Pinioned, of course. One is never quite easy about captives, wouldn't you say? But they can't be helped.'

Appleby was for a moment at a loss. The formidable Lord Ailsworth, whom Colonel Pickering had been so little anxious to approach, had addressed him casually and almost absently, as if here were somebody he was accustomed to meet about the place every day.

'This is Sir John Appleby,' Jean said.

'How do you do?' Lord Ailsworth now advanced with a sort of shy courtesy and shook hands. 'I am always very glad to see Jean's friends.

I should have liked to meet more of her Oxford companions. But we are not much by way of having visitors at Ailsworth, these days.' Lord Ailsworth delivered himself of this in a mildly puzzled manner, as if it were a circumstance of which there must be some obvious explanation that escaped him momentarily. 'Do you come from Oxford yourself?' he asked. 'I get great assistance from the Bureau of Animal Population there. It is much the most important department of the University at present. I myself read Greats, with some emphasis on philosophy. But studies of that sort were already in a decline.'

'I don't come from Oxford,' Appleby said. 'I come from the Metropolitan Police.'

'Yes, of course. How foolish of me.' Lord Ailsworth appeared to judge himself guilty of some discourtesy in not having been better informed about his visitor. But he was not otherwise discomposed. 'Shall we go up to the house?' he asked. 'I hope you can stay to lunch. You mustn't expect roast duck.' This was apparently a joke, and it was accompanied by a smile which somehow made Appleby uneasy. 'But Jean will have explained to you that ours is a vegetarian regimen.'

'When did you last eat roast duck, Grandpapa?' Jean appeared to ask this question quite seriously.

'In 1898, my dear.' Lord Ailsworth gave this reply confidently. 'I remember the occasion very clearly. It was – God help me! – a very *good* roast duck. In fact it gets into my dreams from time to time. Probably roast duck is not what it was. Burgundy is certainly not what it was. Which makes abstention from roast duck the less of a penance. And therefore the less meritorious, it is to be feared.' He touched Appleby lightly and with charming politeness on the arm. 'Let us take this path, my dear sir. No, Jean, you need not carry that basket. I am very capable of managing it myself. I have been taking some cress to the Versicolour Teal. And passing the time of day with our new arrival, the Perry River White-fronted Goose. A charming creature, but rather uncommunicative at present.'

It was obviously desirable, Appleby thought, to find out at once just how mad Lord Ailsworth was. 'You find,' he asked, 'that new arrivals haven't much to say for themselves at first?'

'Quite so, my dear sir. And there is no occasion for your being an exception to the rule.' Lord Ailsworth smiled gently. 'But perhaps I might know whether you are interested in birds? It is something inborn, I think. Certainly I can't remember a time when I didn't know a hawk from a hernshaw.'

It required only a nodding acquaintance with the tragedy of *Hamlet* to realize from this that Lord Ailsworth – superficially at least – had all his wits about him. But it still didn't necessarily follow – Appleby thought – that his madness was only north-north-west. A man can be at the same time extremely acute and extremely crazy. 'I should certainly like to speak up about myself at once,' Appleby said, 'and before trespassing further on your hospitality. It's true that I haven't come because I'm interested in birds. But I have come because it seems probable that somebody else is. I understand that Colonel – '

'Good heavens!' Lord Ailsworth had paused by a pen and now interrupted in some agitation. 'Whatever can have happened to the Wandering Whistling Duck? Fully winged, of course – but very sedentary in habit. And now there's no sign of him. This is most upsetting.'

'Mightn't he' – Appleby ventured to suggest – 'for once be living up to his name? If he's a *wandering* – '

'Precisely!' Lord Ailsworth was becoming more and more excited. 'Sometimes, you know, birds stray out of the reserve and over to the village. They're all scoundrels there – all damnable scoundrels. Particularly at the Bell.'

'At the inn?' Appleby was interested.

'If my fellow magistrates did their duty, that fellow, What's-his-name – '

'Keylock,' Jean said.

'Yes, Keylock. Ought to be under lock and key – eh? Certainly he has no business to be holding a licence. Put anything in the pot – absolutely anything.' Lord Ailsworth was now hurrying forward, apparently intent upon hunting the errant bird. But at the same time he talked on with mounting vehemence and increasing incoherence.

'Weren't we talking about roast duck? Frivolous talk never any good. Real thing on top of you in no time. Apple sauce. I was going on to make a joke about apple sauce. Still possible to have the apple sauce. And something about Burgundy – eh? But Keylock keeps nothing in his miserable tavern except mouldy cheese. So how did he come to be feeding that fellow Juniper on a roast bird? Smell of it all over the place when I went in to talk to him.'

Appleby stopped in his tracks – so uncompromisingly that the others halted too, 'Did you say Juniper?' he asked. 'You are talking, Lord Ailsworth, about Professor Howard Juniper?'

'Yes, that's the man. Put up at the Bell about six weeks ago.'

'But am I not right in thinking that you told the Chief Constable yesterday – '

'Pickering? Tiresome fellow. Do you think I'd admit to young Tommy Pickering that I'd been induced to pay a friendly call on a man who turned out to be eating one of my own ducks?'

'But you're admitting it to Sir John,' Jean said. 'And I'm very glad. I'd like you to go on and tell him all about it.'

'Should you, my dear?' Lord Ailsworth was calming down. 'Why, there he is!' He pointed ahead. A large – and, to Appleby's eye, quite commonplace – duck had turned a corner and was coming sedately towards them. 'Do you know, I think he's struck up a friendship with the Sushkin's Goose? Yes, I believe that is the explanation. Which is a great relief, I'm bound to say. Now, what were we talking about?'

'Howard Juniper,' Appleby said with emphasis.

'Ah, yes. Well I'll tell you all about him at lunch. Interesting chap, in a way. Tolerable, but for his disgusting feeding habits. Had a sense of adventure that's not common nowadays. And intelligent. But that made it all the worse – wouldn't you agree? Stands to reason he knew what that blackguard Keylock had served up to him. However, one oughtn't to speak ill of the dead.'

'The dead?' Appleby was startled. 'You have some reason to suppose that Professor Juniper is dead?'

'Oh, yes. Oh, dear me, yes. Almost sure to be, I'd say. But here we are. I'll show you where to wash, my dear Sir John. Madeira, Jean, would be the right thing, to my mind. Sherry-drinking is overdone these days. And didn't I say something about Burgundy? Capital with nut cutlets. I'll tell Cowmeadow to hunt up a bottle. This way. Water not hot, but privy does flush. Cowmeadow is my butler. My great-grandfather found a lad called Cowmeadow in his regiment of militia. Engaged him as a stable boy at once. And we've had them ever since. Wonderful name – eh? No towel? Too bad. Use my handkerchief.'

Lord Ailsworth was clearly in high good humour, and at the moment it seemed useless to try to penetrate the barrage of his hospitable talk. Appleby contented himself with observing as much of Ailsworth Court as came within his view. Jean's description had prepared him to find the place a vast aviary, and he had rather looked forward to the queer spectacle of some splendid state apartment become the lodging place of the celebrated Tibetan Donkey Ducks. But although a faint persistent susurration in the air did suggest the presence in distant chambers of sundry breeds of lesser fowl, the house as a whole seemed normal in its rather decayed and neglected way.

There was dust but not much cobweb, the carpets were threadbare but not positively treacherous, the large gloomy canvases on the walls were no more indecipherable than they had probably been for a century or more. Cowmeadow when he appeared was indeed excessively shabby, and had much the same encrusted appearance as the bottles of Madeira and Burgundy which he successively produced. The Madeira was of incredible age; the Burgundy, although even half an hour later it was much too cold, could not be accused of the degeneracy that Lord Ailsworth had attributed to its species. The nut cutlets were not, of course, cutlets – but neither, blessedly, did they appear to be compounded of nuts. When Jean was at Ailsworth, Appleby suspected, its domestic economy in general, and its vegetarian diet in particular, were a little tuned up. Lord Ailsworth, although capable of adequately courteous attention to a guest, had little eye for these matters, and every now and then he seemed to withdraw into a dream-world of his own. It wasn't, Appleby hoped as he ate his very reasonable Lenten meal, a dream-world haunted by the phantom savour of fowl hissing on the spit.

Getting back to the subject of Howard Juniper was not easy. Lord Ailsworth, although intermittently talkative on this and that, was elusive about what had happened at the Bell. For a time, indeed, Appleby was inclined to wonder whether his volte-face in point of what he had said to Colonel Pickering the day before might not be the product of a weird sense of humour, and his story of having met Howard Juniper at the inn be a sheer invention designed to baffle the second vexatious irruption of the police that Appleby's visit represented. On the other hand, Lord Ailsworth's invitation to lunch held no trace of anything other than entire good will. Appleby was wondering how to get farther – if indeed there was farther to get – when Jean came briskly and effectively to his assistance.

'Grandpapa,' she said, 'you must tell Sir John all about Professor Juniper. You must tell him at once. Because it seems the matter is very important.'

'The matter of the Garefowl is very important? I quite agree, my dear. But not to our guest. His interest in ornithology is somewhat below the normal, I should say.'

'We don't know what you mean about the Garefowl, Grandpapa. And what is important to Sir John is Professor Juniper. He has disappeared – '

'Quite so. Of course he has disappeared. He couldn't hope to do other than disappear.'

'He has disappeared. And he was engaged, it seems, on very secret work.'

'Quite so, quite so.' Lord Ailsworth was increasingly impatient. 'I know about that. He told me about it. He said, you know, that having to keep his own affairs secret was quite enough, and that he didn't propose to respect similar humbug elsewhere. If they caught him, he said, they were welcome to take a pot-shot at him. That, of course, was nonsense. Or so I suppose. Perhaps if it happened in the dark, and they thought he had come out of a submarine, or something like that, they *might* shoot. Come to think of it, I suppose they *would*. But, you know, he'd never get there. He'd be drowned.'

Appleby had listened to this rambling discourse in steadily deepening astonishment. And what seemed chiefly astonishing was his luck. Unless this excessively eccentric peer was really making the whole thing up, he was on the track of Howard Juniper at last.

'But that is neither here nor there.' Lord Ailsworth seemed to be referring to the supposition that Juniper must have been drowned. 'What startles me, Jean, is your saying that you don't know what I mean by a Garefowl.'

'I said nothing of the sort, Grandpapa. I merely said we didn't know what you meant by starting talking about Garefowl in connexion with this Professor Juniper. I know very well that the Garefowl is the Great Auk. Why, I believe even Sir John knows that. It's the *Alca impennis* of Linnaeus. And it's extinct.'

'Of course it's extinct. It has been for more than a century. But it's true that there has been this rumour. It had quite seized the imagination of this fellow Juniper. I was attracted by him on my afternoon visit, I must confess. But not, I need hardly say, later. Fellow who could devour one of my birds as served up to him by that reprobate Keylock would devour the Great Auk itself, if you ask me. Disagreeable topic, this we've hit on. Let's change it.'

'Not until you've given Sir John a systematic account of the whole affair.' Jean was implacable. 'Or let him ask you whatever questions he thinks necessary.'

'Certainly, certainly. Let him fire away.' Lord Ailsworth spoke with good humour, and turned to Appleby smiling.

Appleby – and it was for the second time – wasn't sure he liked the smile. But at least it seemed as if he were going to get his facts. 'It was specially to see you that Professor Juniper came down to Ailsworth?' he asked.

'I haven't a doubt of it. Although – mark you – he didn't let on that way. He'd heard, no doubt, that we don't at Ailsworth welcome visitors indiscriminately. I ran into him when he was taking a stroll. He had a pair of binoculars and was watching some teal coming in from the estuary. All quite in order; the fellow wasn't trespassing, or showing any signs of it. So I passed the time of day with him. Quite knowledgeable and keen, he turned out to be. I went in to take a cup of tea with him at the Bell.'

'Why – I remember now!' With a confirmatory nod, Jean turned to Appleby. 'Grandpapa mentioned it in a letter – just that he had met somebody and talked birds with him over a cup of tea. It struck me as quite an event in his social calendar. As it would be, wouldn't it, Gran?' And she looked affectionately at Lord Ailsworth.

'No doubt, my dear. But I soon saw that this fellow was after something. Being a very old buffer, you know, and having kept at it for a very long time' – Lord Ailsworth offered a vague gesture which might have been meant to indicate modesty – 'I've made myself something of an authority on the *Alcidae*. And that's what Juniper had in mind. He thought he wanted my opinion. But what he really wanted was to be encouraged in his own. He'd set his heart, if you ask me, on this exploit; and he wanted me to say there might really be something to find at the end of it. Great nonsense, of course.'

'Just what,' Appleby asked patiently, 'is great nonsense?'

'The notion that Garefowl can have appeared and begun breeding on Ardray.'

'Ardray!' Involuntarily, Appleby sat up in his chair.

'I can see you know about the place. Though I'd have thought, Sir John, it was the job of the Navy to guard it, rather than the police.'

'It certainly is. And what started this notion, do you know?'

'A young fellow doing a spell of duty there, I believe. He knew something about birds. And he swore to it. My guess would be that he simply saw some Razor-bills and misjudged the distance and the size. One or two might have aberrant markings above the bill. The lad was killed in a motor accident, shortly after spreading this story. That would give it greater appeal, no doubt. But you can see where the heart of the nonsense lies. Ardray is a prohibited island – rockets or something of the sort – and the story gets a romantic lift, you might say, from that. And it can't be checked up on.'

'But that's monstrous!' With a suddenness that surprised Appleby, Jean was alive with indignation. 'They couldn't exclude properly accredited ornithologists.'

Lord Ailsworth shook his head. 'You forget that the story is nonsense. It *must* be nonsense. No learned society would badger the Admiralty about it. Only a crank would get excited at such a notion. This Juniper was a crank. Highly intelligent, as I said. Leading scientist in his own line. Very interesting line, too. He told me all about it. But a crank, all the same.'

Appleby considered this for a moment. 'These birds,' he asked, 'have just died out?'

The effect of this seemingly harmless question was surprising. Indeed, it might almost have been called alarming. Lord Ailsworth sprang to his feet with a vigour totally unexpected in one of his years. He was quivering with nervous excitement and his eyes were blazing. 'Died out!' he exclaimed in a harsh, high voice. 'Have you been reading the miserable Owen? Have you never heard of John Wolley? Are you unaware, sir, of the criminal folly of your own species?'

There was a moment of silence. Jean made no effort to calm her grandfather. She had gone pale, and was watching him with eyes in which Appleby thought he detected the same haunted expression as he had imagined lurking in them at their first meeting.

'My dear Lord Ailsworth, I do apologize for my ignorance.' There was nothing for it, Appleby decided, except to try to make some soothing remarks himself. 'I quite realize that inept remarks must be very irritating.'

'The apology must be mine.' Lord Ailsworth had sat down again. He was reaching, with a movement that seemed curiously blind, for his Burgundy. But, when he picked up the glass, it was only to thrust it away with a hand that still trembled so violently that the wine was spilt on the table. 'It is the most obstinate of vulgar errors. Sir Richard Bonnycastle, a naturalist almost as great as Wolley himself, exposed it more than a hundred years ago. The Garefowl was murdered, sir, like the Moa and the Dodo. And not by wretched natives seeking food – which was the state of the case with the Donkey Duck until providence allowed me to intervene. Unspeakable blackguards hunted it down in a miserable traffic of eggs and skins.'

'I see,' Appleby said. 'And I can understand it's making you very angry.'

And now Jean did speak. 'There's a vicious circle,' she said, 'in matters of that sort. When creatures are naturally scarce, specimens become valuable. Every beastly museum wants one to stuff and stick in a glass case. So the hunt becomes vigorous. And the fewer the individuals remaining extant, the higher the price it will command. The hunters' effort is progressively stepped up, until not a single specimen is left alive. It's not so bad nowadays, because reputable collectors keep off. But there are plenty of unscrupulous ones. Isn't that it, Grandpapa?'

'Yes, yes – that is it.' Lord Ailsworth produced, with visible effort, the smile Appleby didn't like. 'Let us pass from the subject. Juniper, at least, had no lethal intentions. Or not against birds. But he had them – well, you may say against himself. He was proposing suicide.'

'Suicide?' In his turn Appleby reached for his Burgundy. He was finding Lord Ailsworth hard going. 'Professor Juniper confided to you that he proposed to take his own life?'

'It amounted to that. He had a plan for later in the summer. He proposed to make a dash for the north of Scotland, without letting anybody know, and to go out to Ardray by night. He knew, he said, where he could get hold of a dinghy with an outboard motor. I don't know whether you are acquainted with that coast – '

'I certainly am.' Appleby spoke grimly. 'It's almost unbelievable that he should entertain such a crazy notion.'

'But he *was* crazy.' Again Lord Ailsworth smiled. 'I'm a bit crazy myself, and I should know. There was something entirely freakish in the way the man's mind worked.'

'But didn't you – '

'I simply listened to him in the afternoon. I wasn't quite clear that he was serious. The thing left me, however, very uneasy. That is why I went back in the evening – to do what I could to dissuade him. But, when I found him at that particular dinner, I naturally gave him up.'

Jean was looking at her grandfather in horror. 'How perfectly awful!' she said. She turned to Appleby. 'Is he married? Has he any relations?'

'He isn't married. But he has a twin brother, Miles, who is a schoolmaster. At first I thought it might be Miles who had put up at the Bell. It seems they can pass for one another, they're so alike. But it was the professor, after all.'

'It's a horrible story. Grandpapa, why ever didn't you stop him somehow?'

Lord Ailsworth made no reply. He appeared to have fallen into a sombre reverie.

'I don't think your grandfather could have done much,' Appleby said, 'even if he hadn't been put off by the unfortunate matter of the roast duck. Juniper was a perfect stranger to him, and simply revealed himself as entertaining this dangerous and irrational project. There was no means of restraining him. Lord Ailsworth couldn't lock him up. If Howard Juniper has come to grief – and it looks very much as if he has – the disaster is his own fault.'

'I suppose I *could* have locked him up.' Lord Ailsworth emerged abruptly from his muse, as if lured by this attractive idea. 'Of course I don't sit on the Bench nowadays. But, after all, I am a magistrate. Yes, perhaps I could have committed him. Sent for that young fool Tommy Pickering and had Juniper gaoled for his own good. But there might have been legal repercussions. Things aren't what they were – would you say?'

Appleby wasn't much disposed to attend to this. He drained his wine – it was too good to sacrifice to any emergency – and then asked his host a question. 'I wonder whether I might use your telephone? At once?'

'Certainly, my dear sir. I have no doubt you will want to follow the matter up.' Lord Ailsworth was at his most courteous and normal. 'Indeed, you make me feel I have been very remiss. I could have done something, I am sure. Contacted the poor chap's relations, for example. There is, you say, a schoolmastering brother.'

Jean looked up suddenly. 'That wouldn't be at a place called Splaine something?'

Appleby looked at her in surprise. 'That's right. Splaine Croft.'

'I thought so. I travelled down from Oxford in the same compartment as the schoolmastering brother only the other day. An old pupil of his, Arthur Ferris, was there too. He got Arthur into Rugby. Arthur told me all about him afterwards.'

Lord Ailsworth had risen. 'Interesting but irrelevant,' he said with surprising briskness. 'I'll take Sir John to the telephone.'

7

Appleby got back to London in the late afternoon, drove straight to Burlington House. Among the learned societies accommodated there, the one he sought was not particularly prominent, or even easy to find. But its rooms proved, when attained, to be of very adequate dignity. If the library was small, the books it contained were more than commonly ponderous – being, no doubt, of the resplendently illustrated kind customarily displayed, one at a time, and open upon an improbable lyre-bird, in the windows of the most expensive antiquarian booksellers. Busts and portraits of eminent deceased ornithologists were appropriately interspersed; there was a large glass case containing little piles of small bones – each pile with a handwritten label which had long ago faded into illegibility; over one chimney piece there hung a plaster cast of a fossilized pterodactyl; and over another was an oil portrait of a royal personage playfully holding out a finger to a macaw – the bird being tethered by an improbably massive chain to a black page-boy in the bottom left-hand corner. Appleby, left waiting for a few minutes among all this, thought that there was a smell of aviaries. But the impression must have been a matter of pure suggestion. He wondered whether misguided persons of the simpler classes ever penetrated to these august surroundings in the expectation of receiving a few practical hints on the ailments of budgerigars and canaries.

A little man with a large moustache came hurrying from an inner room. He rather answered to Appleby's idea of Mr Walter Pater. He was dressed in clothes which he might have inherited from a father slightly bigger than himself round about the turn of the century.

'Sir John Appleby? I am Brimblecombe, the Society's Librarian and Secretary. I must apologize for keeping you waiting. We hold our Summer Conversazione next month. It means a great deal of work – a great deal of work on the administrative side. I have just got the cards into the envelopes. Presently I must get the stamps stuck on. I generally do that after tea. A great deal of licking is involved. To be precise, 874 licks. I sometimes think that it might be done with a contrivance – perhaps some sort of sponge.'

'I rather think I've seen something of the sort in post offices.'

'Is that so?' The Librarian and Secretary appeared to be keenly interested. 'Would you mind if I made a note of that? It deserves investigation.'

Appleby indicated his perfect acquiescence in this procedure. 'I hope you didn't mind my ringing up,' he said. 'I'm afraid I've kept you here beyond your usual hour.'

'Not at all, not at all.' Dr Brimblecombe stroked his moustache as a lesser man might stroke his beard. 'I think I understood you to say that you were speaking from Ailsworth. Lord Ailsworth is one of our most distinguished members, I need hardly say. Unhappily, we see very little of him, very little of him, indeed. I entertain not the slightest hope of his attending the Conversazione. You didn't happen to mention it to him?'

'I knew nothing about it, I'm afraid.'

'Ah, no – of course, of course. And how is the dear old man? You said something about the Great Auk, Sir John, that rather alarmed me. If Lord Ailsworth has been inclining his ear to that story, then, I fear, senility cannot be very far off.'

'He regards the rumour about the Great Auk as great nonsense.'

'You relieve me. You relieve me, greatly.'

Appleby smiled. 'And you, for that matter, relieve *me*, Dr Brimblecombe. I take it that there *is* a rumour about the Great Auk?'

'Certainly there is.'

'I had a lurking fear that Lord Ailsworth was making it up.'

Dr Brimblecombe chuckled. 'Quite so. His sense of humour can be very odd. In fact, he is very odd altogether. And as the story about the Great Auk is very odd too, one might well conclude that the former had been the author of the latter.' Dr Brimblecombe paused rather doubtfully, as if wondering whether this had been a perspicuous form of words. 'There appears to be a number of explanations of how this Garefowl story got about.'

'Lord Ailsworth's is that some young man working on Ardray believed himself to have seen the birds. A young man who was later killed in an accident.'

'It may be so. I confess to finding the whole thing very puzzling. And my own suspicion is that it has its origin in a joke or hoax rather than in honest error.'

'There is really no possibility that it is true, Dr Brimblecombe? I remember coming across a book lately which maintained that a good many creatures thought to be extinct can actually be found extant if a search is conducted with sufficient pertinacity.'

'I assure you, Sir John, that nothing of the sort can apply in the present case.' Dr Brimblecombe delivered himself of this with great gravity, and while drawing himself up to his full height of about five feet. 'The Council of the Society would – I have not the slightest doubt – lend its full authority to the statement that the Great Auk is extinct. No intelligent man could review the evidence and believe otherwise.'

Appleby was silent for a moment. 'That sets me a bit of a puzzle, I must confess. And it brings me to my first question. Is Professor Howard Juniper a Fellow – or any sort of member – of your Society?'

'*Howard* Juniper? No, I am sure he is not. But we have a *Miles* Juniper, who is probably his brother. Perhaps you have confused the two?'

'I hope not. We have some evidence that Howard Juniper made rather a hobby of birdwatching at one time. And further evidence that he has kept up, or revived, the interest; and that it took him lately to Ailsworth. But I can take it that he hasn't developed the sort of serious interest in ornithology that would bring him your way?'

Brimblecombe nodded emphatically. 'Certainly you can. If Professor Juniper had even proposed himself as a member, he would have been admitted without question. Indeed, a man of his great scientific eminence would almost certainly have been elected a Fellow, even if he hadn't published papers and so forth in our field. He is, of course, a Fellow over the way.' Dr Brimblecombe made a slightly offhand gesture apparently in the direction of the premises occupied by the Royal Society.

'I see. Well, if his interest in birds was entirely casual and amateur, it is slightly less surprising, perhaps, that he should have taken this Great Auk business seriously.' Appleby frowned, as if this line of thought dissatisfied him. 'Do you think there may be other rare birds on Ardray?'

'No, I don't.' Dr Brimblecombe spoke with sudden vigour. 'One can't devote a lifetime to birds, Sir John, without concluding that the majority have a great deal of sense. And any sensible creature would keep well clear of the island of Ardray nowadays, from all one hears. I'd be much surprised if there are any birds at all. You are no doubt aware that the Council of the Society holds strong views – very strong views – on the complete disregard of ornithological interests in the setting up of experimental stations and proving grounds and test ranges and so forth by the armed forces. In some instances the thing amounts to the wholesale murder of indigenous fauna – nothing less.'

'That is most deplorable, Dr Brimblecombe. Lord Ailsworth, by the way, seems to hold strong views too. You know him personally?'

'Most certainly. We sat on a committee together during the war – a committee set up to advise the Government on ecological warfare.'

'I don't think I ever heard of it. What was the idea?'

'It was thought that pests and so on might be exploited to harass the enemy in areas where the ecological balance was particularly vulnerable. Lord Ailsworth had some startling ideas about the possible rôle of birds.'

'I see. It was a very pretty notion, certainly. Lord Ailsworth was a public-spirited man in those days – keen on winning the war, and so forth?'

Dr Brimblecombe found it necessary to ponder this question. 'He undoubtedly hated the Nazis. He found everything hateful about them – with the exception of their hating us. He felt that, in that particular regard, there was much to be said for their point of view.'

Appleby laughed. 'I've glimpsed that aspect of the old man. Yet he's a mild and courteous person as well. I'm bound to say that this business is bringing me into contact with a lot of queer characters.' Appleby, as he said this, became aware that he was looking at Dr Brimblecombe in a manner that conceivably made the remark somewhat invidious. 'And some remarkable birds too,' he added hastily. 'The Ruddy Shelduck and the Perry River White-fronted Goose.'

'Very interesting,' Dr Brimblecombe said drily. 'But if you contact the Great Auk, I hope you'll let me know.'

Appleby had scarcely got home when he was called to the telephone.

'Miles Juniper here,' said the voice. 'I'm in my brother's confounded laboratory. I suppose this telephone is all right?'

'I'm sure it is. How are you holding the fort?'

'Badly, I imagine. Fortunately they are all as blind as bats down here. You've got no news?'

'I'm afraid I haven't found your brother, if that's what you mean?'

'Then I can't take more of this.' Appleby thought that Miles Juniper sounded genuinely desperate. 'I must have my brother's disappearance announced. I'm more and more convinced that this damned charade is utterly wrong.'

'Could you hold on for another twenty-four hours, Juniper? I did mean to make this evening a deadline, as a matter of fact. But I am on something of a trail now, and I want to have one more go.'

'A trail?' Juniper's voice was suddenly eager. 'Tell me about it, for heaven's sake.'

'Did you know your brother was interested in birds?'

'In birds?' Juniper sounded surprised. 'Well, yes – in a way. Howard was quite keen at one time. Actually, it's been rather more an interest of my own. Why do you ask?'

'Because it's quite certain that, about six weeks ago, your brother treated himself to an expedition to Lord Ailsworth's bird sanctuary. You've heard of the place?'

'Of course I have. I'm a little surprised. But I can imagine Howard's taking a jaunt of that sort into his head. What about it?'

'He met Lord Ailsworth, and told him of a secret plan he had for exploring the island of Ardray.'

'*What!*' Juniper was suddenly astounded. 'I don't think I understand you. Lord Ailsworth told you this?'

'Just so. I suppose you know about Ardray?'

'Let me see. I don't know that I do. Except that it's miles off the west coast of Scotland, and pretty grim. It's absurd that Howard should want to go off there.'

'Not so absurd, it seems, as the reason he gave Lord Ailsworth. He was going to find the Garefowl – the Great Auk.'

'What absolute nonsense!'

Appleby laughed grimly. 'Ornithologically, I gather it's just that. Do you think your brother would know it was just that?'

'I'd be very surprised if he didn't.'

'Do you think it very odd that he should go down to consult Lord Ailsworth on such a project?'

'Of course I do. Damn it, Appleby – talk sense.'

'I'm trying to do just that. And to *think* sense too.' Appleby paused. 'If your brother is too well-informed to find plausible a story that the Great Auk has appeared on Ardray, and if he goes down to Ailsworth for the purpose of proclaiming to an eccentric earl that he *does* find it plausible, and that he is himself going to Ardray to find the creature: well, to just what conclusion does that lead?'

'I don't know. I just don't know.' It seemed to Appleby that Miles Juniper was now a thoroughly bewildered man. 'So I hope, Appleby, that you *do* know.'

'I can only suggest that your brother was leaving a very odd sort of false trail. That, if he had the bad luck to be *caught* on Ardray, there would be an eminent old nobleman to come forward and say it had all been on account of a crazy notion about birds.'

There was a silence – so long that Appleby thought Miles Juniper must have hung up. But nothing of the kind had occurred. 'Sorry,' Juniper's voice said. 'It's just my brain reeling. You're too damned clever, by a long way. But you don't seem to have found Howard, all the same.'

'I'm going to find him.'

'All right. For God's sake do. And I'll keep on with this bloody imposture until this time tomorrow. If all these eggheads don't find me out, that is, and clap me into gaol.'

'Good. And thank you very much, Juniper. I'll be back tomorrow evening.'

'You'll be *back*? You mean you're going to that absurd island?'

'Naturally. I fly there at dawn. The Admiralty won't like it.'

'But that's a mere detail, I suppose?'

'Well, yes. In a matter of this size it certainly is. Goodbye.'

Appleby hung up the receiver and went to join Judith in the drawing-room. She glanced up from a letter she was writing. 'John,' she said at once, 'whatever are you scowling at?'

'Scowling? Am I scowling?'

'Furiously.'

'I'm very sorry, I'm sure. Do I often scowl?'

Judith considered this seriously. 'You scowl when you've made a fool of yourself.'

'I'd call that excusable, more or less. But I haven't been making a fool of myself. At least I'm tolerable sure I haven't.'

'You scowl when you have a nasty sense that something has eluded you.'

'But I don't think – ' Appleby stopped and stared at his wife. 'Yes, you're quite right. I have just that sense. And I've had it once before in this accursed business. It's almost as if – as if somebody had whistled a significant tune, and I'd failed to notice it.'

'A tune?'

'Something like that. It's as if I'd been let down, not by my brains, but by my ear. And I just can't get hold of the thing.'

Judith signed her letter and reached for blotting paper. 'Sleep on it,' she said.

8

Preparing to get out of his aeroplane, Appleby regarded the waiting helicopter with disfavour. 'Have I to get into that thing?' he asked the pilot.

'I'm afraid so, sir. They don't go in for airstrips out on Ardray. I doubt whether there's as much as a bowling green.'

'A bowling green? What would they want that for?'

'All egg heads and boffins out there, except for a few service chaps to look after them. Bowls would be about their mark, I'd say. And badminton for the youngsters in their early fifties.' The pilot smiled cheerfully. 'Jolly game, badminton would be, in an Ardray gale.'

'Gales are the thing out there?'

'Oh, very much so. It's quite supernatural, it seems. Freezing temperatures, howling blizzards and tempestuous seas when the whole of the rest of the Atlantic ocean is like a millpond.'

'You disturb me.' Appleby took another look at the helicopter. 'Do you think it will have – um – a safe driver?'

'Reasonably safe, sir, as long as he doesn't drop off to sleep. Jumbo Brown. A frightful old drunkard, but quite a nice chap. Only reckless when he's been in trouble with women. Of course, he often is. Even up here, I believe – although they brought him north to get him away from them. Jumbo has been ferrying people to and from Ardray for months now. That's why he sometimes drops into a doze.'

'I shall endeavour to combat his somnolence with stimulating conversation.'

'Not under those rotors, you won't. Goodbye, sir. I'm sure you'll have a lovely trip.'

Appleby climbed from the plane. 'Thank you very much.'

'By the way, I'd ask for a parachute, if I were you. They may have one lying around.'

'Thoughtful of you,' Appleby said. 'Goodbye.'

Jumbo Brown provided his passenger not with a parachute but a rug. He tucked him up in this with all the respectful solicitude of an old family coachman.

'I say, sir' – and Jumbo jerked a thumb in the direction of the craft which Appleby had just quitted – 'did they send you north in that?'

'Certainly they did.'

'Criminal, isn't it? Not as if you were an everyday chore, like an Air-Vice or an MP. And was that Batty Tarratt?'

'I understand Tarratt to have been the young man's name.'

'Dear, dear! They've put him on that job, you know, because of his poor tortured nerves. What luck you've had. So far, that's to say. I suppose Batty will take you south again. By the way, did he smell of drink?'

'Certainly not.'

'That's bad. Drink steadies old Batty wonderfully. But when he's keeping off it – well, he just isn't safe. Nice day, isn't it? Of course, we'll bounce about a bit later on.'

Appleby settled himself in his seat. I may be given to scowling from time to time, he was telling himself, but commonly I must have a really nice face. To provoke all this unabashed juvenile fun. Mr Clwyd, now, wouldn't care for it at all.

'All prepared, sir? I just have to wait a signal from the island. Nothing must take off for it from here without the official come-hither.'

'I see. By the way, what about getting there by surface? If I lost my nerve at the sight of your horrible machine, Mr Brown, and insisted on going by water, just what would it be like?'

'Well, sir, it would depend on whether you hit anything.'

'There's plenty to hit?'

'Lord, yes. Not such another piece of water in the world. Littered with wrecks. Viking ships, Spanish galleons, German pocket battleships. Anything you care to name, positively on view from dawn to dusk.'

'Not a part of the world to do a little amateur cruising in?'

'It would depend upon how one felt about heaven, and that sort of thing. St Wulfius must have had a pretty strong line there.'

'St Wulfius?'

'A missionary type, one gathers. Sailed about these waters a long time ago. And had a cell or something on Ardray. Retired there eventually to be an anarchist.'

'An anarchist? How very odd.'

'Or is it an anchorite? Kind of a hermit, you know. And he must have been about the last chap on the island until all this hush-hush got going. Ah, there's my signal. I'd put on the helmet, sir, if I were you. Not one of those noiseless flying hearses, this craft of mine.'

Appleby surveyed the terrain – an activity facilitated by the fact that the floor of the helicopter was for the most part transparent. Apart from the airstrip and its small huddle of sheds, there was no sign of human habitation. In an increasingly crowded world, there are nevertheless spots that are being progressively denuded of inhabitants. And this was one of them. On one of the nearby hillsides, it was true, he could see a thinly spread-out flock of sheep. But the shepherd would come bumping over the moors on a motorbike, perhaps from some clachan a dozen miles away. And the only other irruption, from year's end to year's end, would be by companies of gentlemen concerned to prove their skill at shooting pheasants and grouse. But although it was near the end of August, there was no sign of anybody after the grouse yet. Perhaps there weren't any there to be shot. Perhaps what Dr Brimblecombe called the ecological balance had gone against them.

A helicopter was a very unnatural affair – much more so than an ordinary aeroplane. Perhaps it would be all right if one had done a lot of pioneering with balloons; this business of being sucked straight up above a uniformly widening horizon might then seem entirely unalarming. The contours were already flattening out, but presumably Mr Jumbo Brown wouldn't continue for long to climb in this perpendicular way. Unless, of course, he had dropped off to sleep in earnest. But now there was a change in the note of the engine; the rotorblades were doing whatever they did to ferry one along; the landscape tilted, turned subtly on an axis and began to flow away in a normal-looking fashion beneath them. They were on the way to Ardray.

Appleby wondered why. Another wild-goose chase, he told himself. The quintessential red herring. The perfect turn round Robin Hood's barn. Tomorrow he would find himself back in London – always supposing that Batty Tarratt's poor tortured nerves held out so long – at precisely the point at which he had departed from it.

He paused in his gloomy reflections to take another look at the natural scene. To the east the moors stretched away in unbroken sullen purple to tumble themselves like some unnatural sea against the bastions of the North-West Highlands. And beneath him was a green and racing ocean, tossing itself in spray and spume on jagged rocks, and in one place running far up a golden beach overhung by low cliffs topped with heather. The little boat of St Wulfius, Appleby thought, might with perfect propriety emerge from behind a headland at any moment. For the scene was in all probability utterly unchanged since the ninth century – except that two men were floating through the sky, so securely that they had to keep up boring jokes about their danger, and proposing presently to drop effortlessly upon the remote rock to which the saint could have come only through sheets of foam and past the innumerable submerged fangs of rock that constituted, along with the seethe and suck of small hideous currents, the special hazard of the place.

A dinghy with an outboard motor. Well, Wulfius had certainly had even less than that. But this didn't make Howard Juniper's plan, as reported by Lord Ailsworth, any less ridiculous. A glance at the map showed that mere distance made nonsense of it. Jumbo Brown's helicopter would be more than an hour on the job. No man could seriously have proposed such an exploit. Either Juniper had been romancing to Lord Ailsworth or Lord Ailsworth had been romancing to Appleby. And even suppose that Juniper had in fact had command of some much more powerful craft. It was inconceivable that he could have piloted it, undetected, to one of the most elaborately guarded spots on the surface of the earth. And, if detected, his whereabouts wouldn't be unknown now. On the contrary, Howard Juniper would probably be in gaol. With luck, he might be on bail, with a number of persons quietly keeping an eye on him.

Appleby glanced at Jumbo Brown. The helicopter had every appearance of looking after itself, but it was nevertheless clear that Jumbo's whole being was concentrated on it. A happy man, Appleby thought. Like riding. It's second nature, and you're not thinking about it, and yet you're putting everything you have into it all the time. Happy Jumbo, for whom every wild-goose chase is another jaunt with his enchanting bride. He never makes a fool of himself. Nothing ever eludes him, since the elusive doesn't come his way. And therefore he never scowls.

Appleby scowled. What was eluding him now was any rational occasion for having come here. But perhaps he had never had such occasion. Perhaps he was acting on mere instinct – like Jean Howe's Lemmings. At least, like the Lemmings, he was going straight out to sea. Scotland had virtually cleared off the horizon; had picked up its trailing purple skirts and moved off east. There was nothing to be seen but sea – sea and a few points of leaping white that must mean rock. Round Ardray, he understood, these would be as thick as the hazards on a pin-table. Wulfius must have threaded his way through them with prayer – with that, and a steady hand on the sheet, a steady hand on the tiller.

The sea had turned from green to blue, and then back not to one green but many; from high in the air it was like a strangely veined marble turned molten and seething. Appleby's stomach told him the helicopter was bumping up and down, and less definable sensations seemed best accounted for on the supposition that every now and then it was caught into a sudden lateral drift. Bright sunshine, the uneasy angry sea, a vicious veering wind. A queer part of the world, Appleby had been told. Ardray, thrusting out of the Atlantic, was like a centre round about which the vast forces of wind and water perpetually revolved. But not itself a still centre. Nature, here wheeling and cornering in some mysterious race, reached out a hand in passing and shook the place.

And there it was – a fantastically corrugated basalt mass, rising sheer out of ocean. It was very possibly beautiful, and certainly it was surprising and majestic. But Appleby stared at it almost resentfully. Like almost everything in this Juniper affair, there was no sense to it. How did lava come to behave like that – right out here in the middle of the Atlantic? No doubt the geologists had thought up some answer, but to the lay imagination the island was a massive enigma – as a battleship would be, say, stranded in the middle of the Sahara. And why come to such a remote and sterile spot for the purpose of carrying on ballistic research? Appleby hadn't been given the answer to this puzzle either. He knew only that the place had long been famous as a natural curiosity, and that what was specifically curious about it had proved to be unexpectedly useful. 'You'll find out when you get there,' a very important personage had said to him briskly. 'Murray will show you whatever you want to see. That goes without saying. But I don't see that it can have anything to do with this confounded Juniper and his bugs.'

Appleby didn't see it either. He seemed to see it less and less as the helicopter slowed, hovered, and dropped. Admiral Murray would be waiting for him – having received a signal ordering him so to do. But it didn't follow that it would be with a beaming smile. The man was a scientist. But was said also to be a peppery old sailor who had fought at Jutland. He mightn't welcome a jumped-up policeman talking nonsense about birds.

There was the slightest of bumps. The rotors died and Jumbo Brown whipped off his helmet. 'Space-travel completed,' he said. 'If my calculations have been correct, it's the moon.'

It might well have been the moon, Appleby thought. There was no scrap of vegetation; there was nothing but flat bare wind-whipped rock. Only here and there, he noticed, the surface was broken by what appeared to be small craters – a circumstance which naturally accentuated the lunar suggestion which the place already carried. There were several clumps of low concrete buildings, clinging to the rock like desperate barnacles. And from one of these – it was distinguished from the others by flying an ensign – a small party had just set out, apparently to meet the helicopter. There were some men in uniform and some in what appeared to be the white coats of laboratory workers. Those in uniform held caps jammed on their heads. All were leaning against a howling gale.

The conviction strengthened in Appleby that he was unlikely to be popular on Ardray.

But he turned out to have been quite wrong. This was perhaps because he himself liked the Ardray crowd as soon as Admiral Murray had introduced them to him over a glass of sherry. They were a team with a goal in view. One could imagine them as perched on the edge of the Antarctic continent, organizing for an expedition to the Pole. Only theirs was even more complicated as a co-operative task; they represented a higher percentage of technical accomplishment; and there was – Appleby guessed – an element of danger that lasted longer and was more evenly shared. All this produced a slight effect of the brakes being on so far as the expression of personality was concerned. Everybody was being quiet but not too quiet; one could feel the steady concentration that held these people together day after day and week after week in the pursuit of whatever it was that they had agreed to go after.

As he was led away to lunch in private with the Admiral, Appleby ventured to say something of this impression he had received. Murray looked at him keenly and nodded approval. 'The long count down,' he said. 'If I ever write a book about Ardray – which heaven forfend – I shall call it that. But shall we eat before we tackle business? As I don't have a visitor every day, perhaps you'll indulge me so far. We try to keep a few tatters of civilized habit about us. It's the first thing I tell a new boy when he arrives. Don't only watch your cap. Watch your

119

pants as well. Otherwise the damned gale will have them off you in no time. And, I'm bound to say, I've never had to speak to a chap twice yet. They're a mixed lot, and I don't know that I'd choose all of them to go round the world with. But they're doing me a magnificent job. And we have a very decent chef. Uncommonly rare thing in the services nowadays. I've put more intrigue into nobbling him than into getting my three Fellows of Trinity and my elderly OM. Care to try his game pie? It will be better in October. But it's not bad now.'

Eating game pie, Appleby acquiesced readily enough in half an hour's desultory talk. It was decent of Murray to receive him in this friendly way. 'Does everything have to come to you by helicopter?' he asked, when they had finished their meal.

'Nearly everything does. We do have a harbour of sorts, but it takes some navigating. Nice when you get into it, though – if you can stand the row.'

'The row?'

'Like stage thunder. Whole set-up always reminds me of Covent Garden. If you don't mind being blown about, we'll go and have a look.'

They left the Admiral's hut and were at once standing on the bare windswept rock. 'No hope of raising your own vegetables,' Appleby said.

'Decidedly not. Backside of the world, I call it. How does it go? Ever-threatening storms of Chaos blustering round, and so forth. Great poet, Milton – despite his damned bad politics. Mind a ladder, Appleby?'

Appleby intimated that he didn't mind a ladder. He had been led past two of the queer craters with which the flat surface of the island was pitted, but he hadn't been invited to inspect them. Instead, he was guided to the eastern extremity of Ardray, where the sheer cliff which everywhere else constituted its perimeter appeared to break down into a narrow cleft. This itself almost immediately became perpendicular, and appeared to have been adapted to serve as something like the shaft of a lift. There was a steam winch with a naval rating guarding it, and from an iron gantry cables disappeared into near-darkness below. So did a narrow iron ladder, clamped into the rock. The Admiral slung an electric torch on a lanyard round his neck, and went down without a word. Appleby, under the friendly but slightly ironical eye of the rating, followed with amateur circumspection.

The torch was needed only during the middle section of the descent. After that there was daylight again – but of a quality so unusual that Appleby judged the comparison with Covent Garden to be quite in order. The cave into which the cleft dropped seemed at first to be a great pillared hall with a floor of green marble. But the floor was water, and the pillars – red and brown and green and gold – were nature's handiwork alone; massive basalt formations, fantastically hung with seaweed and lichen. Appleby, finding his feet at length on firm rock, looked round at his leisure. The sea, he saw, was in soft perpetual movement up and down. It must be this that was responsible for the sound – as of a vast creature gently breathing – with which the place was filled.

'The Hermit's Chapel,' the Admiral said. 'You may have seen the same sort of thing on Staffa. Curious, isn't it?'

Appleby agreed that it was curious. At the same time, he reflected with a faint impatience that it wasn't as a tourist that he had come to Ardray. The sights were, as they say, well worth a visit. But they didn't seem to bring him any nearer to Howard Juniper. 'The hermit,' he said, 'being Wulfius?'

'Certainly. And perfectly historical, you know. Not a doubt about him. Great man. Sailed these seas as if they were a duck pond. There was a move to call our brainchild the Wulfius. But I wouldn't have it. Inappropriate. Blasphemous, almost. Or in howling bad taste – which is, of course, worse.'

'Your brainchild? The project you're all working on?'

'Yes, yes. I'll show it to you presently. Glad to have somebody it *can* be shown to.'

Appleby was still looking round the cave. 'But you don't work down here?'

'Lord, no. But it's useful. We can get craft in at low tide. On the less stormy days, that is. At other times it would be uninhabitable. Extraordinary effects from compressed air. They deserve study – or would in a sane world. That produces the terrific row I was speaking of. Sorry you can't hear it.'

'This is quite striking enough. By the way, what *did* you decide to call the brainchild?'

The Admiral chuckled. 'Come and see one or two of them,' he said. 'Then I'll give you three guesses.'

They went back up the ladder. Appleby was glad to see the end of it. 'Probably,' he said, 'I'd need more than three guesses to get at why you're all here at all. It can't be just for privacy. And all the transport must make it enormously expensive.'

'You're in the target-area – but actually barking up precisely the wrong tree.' Murray was now striding across the island. 'Enormously expensive is just what it's not. The point about Ardray is that Mother Nature has done a big preliminary job for us, absolutely gratis. Just go carefully, will you? Up to the edge and peer over.'

They had reached one of the craters which had been among Appleby's first observations on the island. It proved to be a natural shaft of not more than eight yards in diameter. It seemed to Appleby not informative. It was a mere pit of blackness.

'Not in use, this one,' Murray said. 'Drop something.'

Appleby found a loose fragment of rock and dropped it. He listened. 'Good lord!' he said.

'Quite a tidy depth – eh? We'll go on to the next.'

They walked on about twenty paces. The next shaft had a low fence round it. A number of pipes and wires ran up to its lip and disappeared.

'Air and so on,' Murray said. 'Nobody down there now. But we've got one of *them* there. Just take a look.'

Again Appleby peered down. As he did so, Murray stooped and flicked a switch. The black pit was instantly illuminated. At the bottom it was probably a good working light. But from the bright daylight above it gave only an uncertain view.

'Well, what do you see?' Murray was whimsically challenging.

'Nothing very clearly,' Appleby said. 'But at least I think I see the idea. It's this business of getting off rockets from very deep underground, isn't it? Absolute invulnerability for the launching of thermonuclear jobs?'

Murray nodded soberly. 'Just that. And here, on Ardray, a devilishly inscrutable providence, Appleby, has provided us with a dozen or more of these infernal pits ready-made – just by way of encouragement.'

'Mysterious,' Appleby said drily.

'Just that. Fortunately, the real problems are left for us to solve. And they're enormous, as you can imagine. Doing the sums, and all that, keeps us sane. If we *are* sane, which I sometimes take leave to doubt. But look again, will you? There's a little fellow down there now.'

Appleby looked again. 'Yes, I see. But I don't know I'd call it all that little.'

Murray chuckled. 'How would you describe it?'

Appleby shook his head. 'I really can't make much of it, in this violently foreshortened aspect. But I'd describe it as a dumpy pear-shaped object, with what look like rather ineffective flippers halfway up.'

'Capital!' Admiral Murray was delighted. 'You've caught the essence of it very nicely. And that, you know, is why I've christened it as I have. Not that "christen" is perhaps the right word. Another piece of confounded blasphemy, come to think of it.'

Appleby turned and stared at his host. He wasn't going to need three guesses. 'Would I be right,' he asked, 'in supposing that you've named the thing after an earlier visitor to this island?'

'Absolutely right. Brilliant shot, if I may say so. The Great Auk it is.'

'Well,' Appleby said when they had returned to the Admiral's office, 'at least I know now how this rumour about Garefowl on Ardray got around. Incidentally, the thing would make quite a good study of how rumours augment themselves as they travel. Have you heard the version about the young man who was working for you here, who believed himself to have seen the birds, and who was later killed in an accident?'

Murray shook his head. 'That's a new one to me. But I do know that my modest flight of fancy has caused confusion. If I'd just dubbed the thing the Pink Streak or the Grey Crusader or something like that, no excitement would have been caused. But of course the fellows who know about birds wouldn't be taken in for a moment. Come to think of it, I wish I'd called it the Golden Eagle.'

Appleby laughed. 'Wouldn't you have done better still to call it the Dodo?'

'In the hope that a little rationality in the world might render it obsolete? But the Great Auk carries that idea too.' Abruptly, Murray dropped this vein of whimsy. 'Well, now – what have you come about?'

'About a fellow who may be described as in another branch of your lethal trade, and who has very awkwardly vanished. His name is Howard Juniper.'

Murray sat up straight 'Vanished! Howard Juniper? I'm most concerned to hear it. I know him quite well.'

'The dickens you do!' Appleby sat up in turn. 'And do you imagine he knows you work here?'

'Certainly he does. Why, I had dinner with him the last time I was in London. That's about two months ago.'

'Did you talk about birds?'

Murray shook his head emphatically. 'I'm sure we didn't. Why should we?'

'Well, it seems that Juniper was interested in them at one time. Do you know that as a young man he went in for extravagant hoaxes, and so on?'

'I believe I've heard of it. But I shouldn't suppose him to be much by way of that sort of thing now.'

'Would it surprise you to learn that, shortly after you last met him, he was meditating a plan to make a secret raid on Ardray?'

'It would.' For the first time, Admiral Murray spoke a shade testily. He plainly thought the conversation was veering into nonsense.

Appleby caught the note. 'I'm sorry,' he said, 'to ask all these idiotic-seeming questions. But, I assure you, it's not for fun. Do you know Lord Ailsworth?'

'Ailsworth? I seem to have heard the name. No more than that.'

'He's not a person of any prominence, except among ornithologists.'

Murray made an impatient gesture. 'For heaven's sake! We keep on coming back to birds. What's this supposed to be in aid of?'

'Discovering Howard Juniper – which it's vitally necessary to do. As you must know, his line is bugs. Stopping bugs. Starting bugs. Teaching bugs to turn inside out when he whistles to them. And any other damned crazy thing.' Appleby was impatient in his turn. 'And he told this Lord Ailsworth – if this Lord Ailsworth is to be believed – that he was coming to Ardray. He said he was coming to Ardray in a dinghy, as a matter of fact.'

'Did he, indeed!' The Admiral, it seemed to Appleby was becoming quite ominously red round the neck.

'Just that. He went down to Ailsworth, got hold of this odd old fellow who's mad on birds, and told him he was coming in a dinghy to Ardray to find the Great Auk. He was convinced that the bird was still extant, and that the rumours were of something that had authentically happened. What do you make of that?'

'I make something perfectly clear of it.' Murray had calmed down again. 'Lord Ailsworth is *not* to be believed. He's been spinning you a fairy story. It's not my business to tell you why. But I suppose it must be out of a misjudged sense of humour. Or as a consequence of sheer lunacy.'

'I have independent testimony that Juniper did go down to Ailsworth about six weeks ago. And I have the evidence of a thoroughly reliable girl that the old man – if only in general terms – reported the meeting to her at the time.'

'Well, it's all your puzzle. But I repeat that Howard Juniper didn't tell this precious nobleman of yours that he believed in the rumour about the Great Auk.'

Appleby was silent for a moment. 'May I ask,' he said mildly, 'how you can be so positive?'

'Yes, of course you can – although I suppose that the answer convicts me of an indiscretion. I wasn't quite accurate when I said that Juniper and I didn't talk about birds. In a manner of speaking, that is. I told him what it was reasonable to tell him about our work here. And I mentioned my fancy for calling our confounded missile the Great Auk. He certainly took it in. I'd say he was rather tickled. In other words, Appleby, one of the few men in England who *couldn't* believe the rumour about the actual bird's being extant was and is Howard Juniper.'

In the bleak silence that succeeded this there was a tap at the door and a rating came in. 'Radio telephone for Sir John Appleby, sir.'

Murray pointed to a telephone on his desk. 'Here,' he said.

'Aye aye, sir.'

A moment later the instrument buzzed. Appleby picked it up. 'Appleby?' said a rumbling voice.

'Yes.'

'Clandon here. Glad they've run you to earth. Will that line of yours be scrambled?'

'Certain to be. Go right ahead.'

'The usher's vanished.'

'What's that?' For a moment Appleby could make no sense of this remark.

'Your spurious professor. Your blasted Miles Juniper. Disappeared into thin air. First Howard and then this schoolmaster. Do you read Wordsworth? How fast has brother followed brother, from sunshine to the sunless land. I don't know what you've gone rushing off about to Ultima Thule, or wherever you are. But I think you'd better return to civilization and clear this matter up.'

'All right,' Appleby said. 'I will.'

9

It was just after midnight when Appleby got back to Scotland Yard. Cudworth appeared in his room almost at once. Between attending to reports, he had been pacing his own room restlessly for hours.

'Grindrod,' Cudworth said. He pronounced the name not quite impassively. It was, for him, a highly dramatic performance.

Nevertheless it was a moment before Appleby registered the name. He had been sunk in thought. 'Grindrod?' he repeated. 'What about him?'

'He's in on this affair. In fact, he's behind it.'

Appleby frowned impatiently. 'I don't know what affair you're talking about, or why it should be keeping you here at midnight. And I don't want to hear about it, Cudworth. The Juniper business is quite enough for me at the moment.'

Cudworth stared. 'But I'm talking about the Juniper business. Karl Grindrod, certainly one of the greatest rascals outside gaol in this country at the present moment, is quite certainly involved.'

'Rubbish! I don't believe a word of it.'

Cudworth stopped staring and looked angry. 'Do I understand, sir, that you wish me to take no further part in this particular case?'

Appleby sat down rather heavily. 'I'm sorry, Cudworth. This rushing around in aeroplanes can't agree with me. I know Grindrod is, in the abstract, a likely man. He's strongly suspected of having had a hand in two or three quite tidy espionage jobs in the last couple of years. The sooner he's locked up the better. All I ought to have said is that what you tell me appears very unlikely. Perhaps I oughtn't even to say that. The fact is simply that the Juniper puzzle is at last beginning to arrange itself more or less coherently in my head. I'm prepared to say I've almost got the hang of it, although it's quite unbelievably rum. And nobody like Grindrod has any place in the picture. But do please tell me what's turned up.'

'That's all right, sir.' Cudworth was quickly mollified. 'When I got your instructions from that island I went down to the laboratories at once. It appeared that Mr Miles Juniper had walked out on his job – I suppose I ought to say his brother's job – just after you had a telephone conversation with him yesterday evening.'

Appleby nodded. 'That doesn't surprise me at all. In fact, it fits in nicely with the fact that *I* surprised *him*. I told him something that astounded him. The whole picture I'm building up turns on that, I may say.'

'May I know what your picture is, sir?'

'Well, Cudworth, perhaps not quite yet. You might want to have me certified – which would be a shame, if I'm really beginning to get on top of this damned thing. I'll just say that this bolt from the laboratories is quite satisfactory to me. Now, go on.'

'I found Dr Clandon in a great state, and cursing somebody he called the usher. Old word for a schoolmaster, it seems. He meant Miles Juniper. He supposed that Miles' nerve had simply failed, and that he'd dropped the imposture you'd set him to and bolted. His line – Dr Clandon's, that is – was that your bright idea had done no good, would probably cost him his job, and ought to cost you your job, too.'

Perhaps for the first time since leaving Ardray, Appleby smiled. 'Clandon let you have all this – and perfectly good-humouredly?'

'Well, yes.' Cudworth appeared surprised at this piece of knowledge on Appleby's part. 'Dr Clandon was very upset, but you might say that he was making the best of it. Then I gave him your message. I said that in these changed circumstances the disappearance of Professor Juniper would have to be made public without further delay, and that his senior colleagues should be given the full story at once. So he had in half a dozen of them, there and then, and explained the matter. They weren't too pleased.'

'They wouldn't be, I'm afraid. But I'm sure *you* were, Cudworth. Here were half a dozen fresh people to put through your routine.'

'Just that, sir.' Cudworth spoke impassively. 'And I got results. Of course I had my photographic files in the car – I seldom go about without them – and I had them in. So I started with the foreign agents and their principal contacts. And when Grindrod's ugly mug turned up, I got two separate recognitions straight away. And – it seems to me – in an uncommonly significant relationship. One of these fellows said he had seen Grindrod present himself on the previous evening at Professor Juniper's room. Of course I checked up at once with junior staff, and it seemed perfectly true. Grindrod had appeared, sent in a note to Professor Juniper – to the *supposed* Professor Juniper, that is to say – and got an interview straight away. It lasted about fifteen minutes.'

Appleby had got up and walked to his uncurtained window. For a moment he appeared absorbed in the lights of a police launch going down the river. 'And this would be just before Juniper telephoned to me?'

'Yes, sir. That gets the timing exactly.'

'Telephoned to me in some agitation, saying he couldn't carry on longer with what he called the damned charade, or some such phrase. It begins to make a picture, Cudworth, I agree. That it isn't quite the picture I've been making myself is beside the point. Well, go on.'

'Another of the fellows called in by Clandon had actually seen Professor Juniper – the *supposed* Professor Juniper – leave the laboratories. That was about half an hour later again. Juniper had simply hailed a taxi and gone off, taking nothing with him. So this fellow thought nothing of it. Nobody did, until Clandon discovered today that Juniper had vanished without explanation. But the immediate point is this. The chap who saw Miles Juniper – *our* Miles Juniper – go off in this way, saw a car draw out from the side of the road and follow the taxi. Again, he thought nothing of it. But he did recognize in Grindrod's photograph the man at the wheel.'

'I see.' Appleby had turned back into the room. 'It's a very pretty sequence, certainly.'

'Yes, sir. Professor Juniper has vanished, and his brother Miles is – as you might say – keeping up appearances. Grindrod – whose reputation we know – calls on Miles. Miles is upset, and rings you up in obscure agitation. Miles bolts. Grindrod proves to have been lurking around, and follows. Miles doesn't turn up again.' Cudworth paused, evidently pleased with this succinct statement. 'And there's one other significant fact.'

Appleby nodded. 'I'm sure there is. You have, you know, in your subtle way, a fine sense of climax. Let's have it.'

'I don't know about that.' Cudworth looked rather suspiciously at Appleby. 'But this further fact jumped out at me as soon as Grindrod swam into the picture and I had a more thorough look at his record. Of course there was a good deal of it that I had in my head. A dangerous chap. First turned up in an obscure affair just before the war. Shot a man called Shergold – and undoubtedly in self-defence. Pitched a yarn that it was straight jealousy stuff about a woman. But we suspected that Shergold was going after him with his own gun because Grindrod was blackmailing him.'

'I remember all that. And didn't Grindrod then disappear?'

'He disappeared abroad, all right. It was the sensible thing to do. And his next adventure was probably treason. A nice quiet war in Germany, giving Goebbels a helping hand from time to time. But the end of it found him more or less innocently in Spain, and there was nothing definite enough to base a charge on. Since then, he's just kept us wondering. But the significant fact I noticed in his record dates from farther back than all that.'

'An association with one or other of the Junipers?'

'With both of them, sir. And very early on. They were all three at the same public school and the same Cambridge college.'

'That's certainly something. You wouldn't know whether your precious rascal was in the Cambridge boat?'

Cudworth found this question mildly surprising. 'I've no record of it.'

'Or played Rugger for England?'

'I don't know. But I could easily find out.'

'Perhaps it isn't important. At least we can say that he rubbed shoulders with our Howard and Miles quite a lot. And that he has shown a sudden revived interest in them.'

'Well, sir, a revived interest in Howard. And, of course the significance of his early association with the brothers at school and college is obvious. He would know of their old amusement of exchanging identities. And he might well be especially able to distinguish between them. So consider the situation yesterday. Grindrod seeks out Howard – probably for no very honest purpose. He is shown in on the man purporting to be Howard. And – either instantly or after a few minutes – he sees that it isn't Howard, but Miles. Miles realizes that his impersonation is discovered, and is upset. He is so upset that presently he bolts. But Grindrod, who realizes that he is on to a good thing, has lurked about, and now follows him. I'd put my money on all that. But I'm blessed if I can see where it leads us.'

'To the missing brother, I hope.'

'Well, I hope so too, sir. It seems a more promising trail than your trip to Ardray. I can't think very much came of *that.*'

'Not much ought to have come of it, I agree.' Appleby saw that Cudworth's cavalier reception at the beginning of the interview still slightly rankled with him. 'But, as a matter of fact, something did. Sheer luck at the end of a hunch, you might call it. Of course I confirmed the fact that anybody's making a secret trip out there is nonsense. But I could have done that without taking to the air. The luck was in something that I got, almost casually, from the top man there. And it slewed the whole case round for me. They call the damned thing they're fooling about with on that island the Great Auk. And Howard Juniper knew that. So either Juniper was romancing to Lord Ailsworth or Lord Ailsworth has been romancing to me. The latter, I think. But now we're going to find out. Get a car round. And ring up Clandon and have him out of his bed. We'll collect him on the way, and be at Ailsworth for breakfast.'

'Ailsworth?' Clandon said, as the car ran rapidly through deserted streets. 'I suppose I've met him. My father knew him pretty well, before he retired from the world and went dotty on birds. Harmlessly and deeply mad, I understand. I'm sceptical about his having much to do with our problem.'

'So is Cudworth,' Appleby said. 'But put it this way. Chronologically, and so far as our record goes, the problem begins with Ailsworth and at Ailsworth. It begins more or less on solid ground there, and only sails into the blue thereafter. Howard Juniper – although to a lesser extent than his brother Miles – has an interest in birds. So he treats himself to a little holiday down at Ailsworth, where birds are to be observed in plenty. Nothing odd in that. It's true that he practises a totally unnecessary petty deception, telling some story about an appointment in Edinburgh. But people on work like his do get irked by the sense of being on a string. Wouldn't you agree?'

'Great God, yes.'

'Very well. Howard has a day or two down there, including what appears to be a chance encounter with Lord Ailsworth. And then he returns to work. There's nothing odd in the episode except the yarn that Ailsworth himself spins about it: Howard Juniper's divulging his intention of going to Ardray to hunt the Great Auk. We now know positively that he couldn't genuinely have had any such plan, since he happened to know that the Great Auk is a missile and doesn't lay eggs. So we come to our first question, which I was putting to Cudworth a little time ago. Who is telling a lie? The only motive I can find for Howard Juniper's doing so seems quite fantastic: he was going out of his way to contact Ailsworth for the purpose of laying some sort of false trail. But why Ailsworth? The old man lives a more retired life than almost anybody in England, and his meeting with Juniper might never have come to light at all. So I accept, tentatively, the other interpretation. It was Ailsworth who was laying a false trail. He wanted to get rid of me. The old rumour about the Great Auk, or Garefowl, on Ardray came into his head, and he promptly spun me this yarn about his meeting with the man who subsequently disappeared. Of course it's thoroughly queer – but, granted Ailsworth's eccentricity, it's not implausible.'

'It's not implausible, certainly.' Cudworth spoke from the wheel of the car. 'But it isn't intelligible. It leads us nowhere.'

'Sir John appears to think it does.' Clandon, engaged in lighting a large curly pipe, rumbled contentedly. 'Back to Ailsworth, it seems. At least it looks as if it may be a nice day for an outing. But go on.'

Appleby nodded. 'Very well. But I agree that here is, for the moment, a dead end. Lord Ailsworth's romancing doesn't make sense in terms of any information we've reviewed so far. So go on to the next thing: the real start of the case. Somebody vanishes.'

'Quite so. And surely – ' Clandon checked himself. 'Would you say that again?'

'Somebody vanishes.'

'There's nothing like caution.' Cudworth, as he offered this reflection, somewhat inconsistently relieved his feelings by swinging the car hazardously round a bend. 'Somebody vanishes. But we mustn't say who. It may have been Professor Juniper. But it may have been Charley's Aunt. Or the Abominable Snow Man. Or – '

'Or *Miles* Juniper.' This time, Clandon didn't rumble. He snapped. 'It's an idea. Yes, it's a point of departure, undeniably. But it certainly invites us to abandon solid ground and ascend into that blue like a rocket. In fact, I never heard anything so bizarre in my life. In heaven's name, Appleby, what should put such an idea in your head?'

'Something, as a matter of fact, that has been haunting my ear obstinately from the start of the affair. I'll tell you in a minute. But answer me this question first. What has been your main impression of the chap you've been passing off during the last few days as Howard Juniper?'

'I've told you already. That he's been a damned bad actor. Trying to back up your crazy scheme, my heart's been in my mouth a dozen times. The fellow couldn't act his brother for toffee.'

'And why not?'

'Why not!' Words seemed to fail Clandon. 'Because as I say, he was a damned bad actor. We're talking in a circle.'

Appleby chuckled. 'You may be. I'm not. Think of the history of the Junipers. They made a hobby from boyhood of their peculiar brand of Box and Cox. And they were both experienced amateur actors. Why should Miles come so near to muffing the thing when he addressed himself to it in your blessed research establishment? I can see only one answer. Because he wasn't Miles at all. He was Howard.'

'My dear Appleby, I never heard such a preposterous piece of false logic. Surely – ' Clandon stopped abruptly, and stared at his companion. 'Or did I?'

'Exactly. There's nothing wrong with the logic of the thing, whatever we may think of its common sense. Howard had to impersonate himself. More strictly, and so far as you were concerned, he had to play the part of Miles Juniper called upon to play the part of Howard Juniper. And he *was* Howard Juniper. It was a situation that would tax the most accomplished of professional actors, I imagine. And Howard – for we are talking about Howard, remember – overplayed the factor of error. I don't know whether that's the apt expression, but you see what I mean. Howard's real difficulty was that you might see he was *Howard*. Shall we turn to another thing?'

'Turn to anything you like.' Clandon, although the chill of the early morning was yet in the air, produced a large silk handkerchief and mopped his brow.

'Then consider this. What really staggered the man I saw at Miles Juniper's prep school was the suggestion that his missing brother might have carried off with him some unspeakably lethal stuff from your laboratories. He was still, according to your own observation, in a state of great uneasiness during the first evening of his impersonation – if impersonation is the right word for it. On the following morning he was – as I think you expressed it – another man. Now, suppose Miles to have been, for some reason, playing the professor – while the professor, correspondingly, was playing the schoolmaster. Miles would naturally have access to whatever was about the place. If Howard had grave apprehensions about Miles' nervous stability, and had at the same time allowed this whole prank or whatever it was to go forward, he would naturally be in acute anxiety in case Miles, in disappearing, actually *had* taken something quite appalling away with him. But this would be something that Howard could check up on as soon as he had the run of his own laboratory again in private. And – in the existing circumstances, and short of an actual confession of the whole extraordinary situation – he could get that run of his own laboratory only by falling in with my proposal that he should, for a few days, take on the rôle of his brother' – Appleby smiled wryly – 'or of the man I *thought* was his brother.'

Intent on a fast trip, Cudworth made one of his few interruptions. 'A little loosely phrased, that one,' he said. 'But we follow you.'

'Thank you. Well, the reason that Howard impersonating Miles impersonating Howard cheered up on the following day must have been because he had discovered that nothing particularly deadly was, in fact, missing.' Appleby glanced at Clandon. 'Would that fit?'

'As well as anything else in this nightmare. But we don't yet know why the brothers should change identities in the first place, or why Miles while impersonating Howard should disappear, or why Howard impersonating Miles impersonating Howard should also disappear, or why Lord Ailsworth should have anything to do with it, or where this fellow, What's-his-name – '

'Grindrod.'

'Or where Grindrod comes into the story at all. And you haven't told us, Appleby, what really set you on this extraordinary line of elucidation – if it *is* elucidation – in the first place.'

'Consider this. The boys at Splaine Croft believe that their headmaster, although in various ways an admirable person, particularly with a cricket ball, is an ambitious man, disappointed and a bit messed up. Boys are commonly acute in discerning a matter of fact of that sort, although they may go quite astray in assigning reasons for it. Add the point that Miles Juniper is *vain*. It was my wife who got hold of that. He is an entirely obscure schoolmaster, and not particularly wealthy. But his house contains an oil portrait and a bronze bust of Miles Juniper which between them must have cost two or three thousand pounds. That's not normal, surely. The man's neurotic. And he has one quite freakish symptom which his famous and successful brother Howard occasionally allows him to indulge. Just that of *being* Howard.'

Clandon used his handkerchief again. 'It's devilishly plausible, I must say.'

'And vice versa?' Cudworth asked.

Appleby took a moment to consider the bearing of this Latinism. 'Well, yes. It would be my guess that Howard is the stronger and more stable, as well as the more talented, brother. I felt a basic strength in him, at our first meeting.'

'When supposing him to be Miles,' Cudworth said, rather unnecessarily.

'Quite so. And when he was supposing me to be somebody called Clwyd.' Appleby suddenly laughed aloud. 'It must have tickled him – wouldn't you say? – finding himself visited by somebody pretending to be somebody else. But to get back to what I was saying. Howard is the stronger and more stable – but like many strong and stable people, he probably pushes himself well up to his nervous limit. The little comedy of retreating for a few days from time to time into the obscurely beneficent rôle of a prep-school master was no doubt a pleasure to him. So it *is* probably vice versa, as Cudworth says: there's a mutual satisfaction in the manoeuvre. Of course in psychological terms there is no doubt a good deal more to it than that. A compulsive neurosis, established on the basis of nursery pranks. It's a wonderful subject for investigation.'

Clandon gave his rumbling laugh. 'Always supposing it isn't moonshine, my dear chap. But you haven't yet really told us what set you on all this.'

'Something extremely simple. There was a point during my first interview with Howard impersonating Miles – at Splaine, that is to say – at which Howard nearly betrayed himself. He began to say "Is it about Miles?" And then he checked himself, and managed to make it "Is it about my brother?" instead. But the thing, as I've said, had been just perceptible to the ear – and it hung on my ear, so to speak, without finding the way into my mind. Much later, when the common noun "miles" turned up in Howard's conversation on a telephone line, the perception just prickled at me again. And then, a good deal later again, it suddenly got through. The man I had unquestioningly taken to be Miles Juniper, and whom I had *asked* to be Howard Juniper, *was* Howard Juniper. Unless I was achieving a quite false recollection, there could be no other explanation.'

Clandon looked dubious. 'What,' he asked, 'about that psychopathology of everyday life stuff? Ending a letter with "I hope you are still dead" when you ought to be writing "I hope you are still in your customary rude health". Wouldn't something of that sort cover Miles calling Howard Miles? Freud has a lot to say about such slips of the tongue. And, after all, you are hard at work putting the brothers Juniper into some sort of psychopathological category anyway. Twins nipping into each other's jobs. Pity they're not married. You can imagine all sorts of high jinks – '

Cudworth blew an unnecessary blast on his horn. He was a man, Appleby knew, who deprecated coarse pleasantries. 'Supposing,' Cudworth said, 'that this extraordinary substitution really took place, and that the disappearances have been successively of Miles impersonating Howard and of Howard impersonating Miles impersonating Howard, how does Lord Ailsworth come in? And how does Grindrod come in? If your theory is correct, sir, Grindrod didn't do what I was suggesting he did. He didn't, that is, detect that Howard was really Miles. Because Howard wasn't Miles. Howard was Howard, although *we* thought him Miles.' Cudworth paused in exasperation. 'It's almost impossible to keep all this straight as one talks. But I'm asking about Lord Ailsworth and Grindrod. Who have they believed to be who?'

'In short,' Clandon demanded, 'what the devil is it all about?'

Appleby glanced at his watch. 'I hope,' he said, 'that we shall have all the answers by lunchtime.'

PART THREE

JUNIPER AND JUNIPER

1

Miles Juniper looked up from the bench on which he was slumped and recognized his brother. 'Look out!' he cried. But it was too late. The stout door had slammed to and the bolts slid into place. The footsteps of Lord Ailsworth could be heard descending to ground level at leisure. He was resting on his labours for the time being.

Howard Juniper was not unduly alarmed. He ought not to have let this happen. Knowing and suspecting what he did, he ought decidedly to have been more on his guard. But he was clear that he wasn't going to take Lord Ailsworth seriously. Miles, no doubt, had done so. And Lord Ailsworth, thus encouraged in melodrama, had kept the outrageous nonsense up for days.

Howard looked about him coolly. Having found Miles – a Miles whom a glance showed to be unhurt although sulky and frightened – his anxieties abruptly diminished. 'Remote – isn't it?' he said almost casually. It was the manner he always found useful in coping with Miles.

'Of course it's remote.' Miles sat up and stared at his brother – at once resentfully and with enormous relief. 'Nobody's allowed near this tower except the old imbecile himself. He has maps and things upstairs, which is his excuse for keeping it all locked up. There's another and smaller tower for his assistants.'

'So I gathered. Have you tried shouting?'

'Of course I've tried shouting.'

But not very hard, Howard thought. Miles always has lacked pertinacity. Aloud, he said cheerfully: 'Let's shout together. That will be twice the racket.'

141

'I don't think we'd better. He might come back in a rage and blow our brains out.'

'Rubbish, Miles. He's an irresponsible old lunatic, clearly enough. But I see not the slightest reason to suppose him homicidal.'

'Don't you, indeed?' Miles seemed to find this very funny. He laughed in a sharp hysterical way his brother didn't care for. 'Ailsworth's ambition, if you want to know, is simply to be the champion homicide of all time. That's what this is about.'

'Well, well – think of that.' Howard was determinedly amused. 'I find that decidedly helpful. It introduces sense in the affair. A madman's sense of course. But that's better than none. As summer quarters, I find this quite snug. Rugs, I see. But doesn't he provide his guest rooms with books?'

'Funny, aren't you?'

Howard couldn't remember a time when Miles, in his feeble spells, hadn't been in the habit of coming out with that bitter question. Of course Miles was by no means always feeble. It was just something that came on him. 'And sanitation?' he asked.

Miles pointed to a small trapdoor in the floor. 'All mod cons,' he said with a sudden grin. 'And there's another trapdoor up there.' He pointed to the stout wooden ceiling. 'That's the map room. He lowers food down. Brings it in a basket, along with watercress for his favourite birds. And talks and talks – through that hole.'

'Very odd, indeed.' Howard sat down with an air of placid comfort on a bench. 'I'm afraid, you know, that after this we'll have to drop it.'

'Drop it?'

'Brothers through the Looking-Glass. It doesn't square with my confounded job nowadays. Mind you, Miles, I like being Miles Juniper now and then. I like Splaine. I like the boys. But I don't like' – Howard's voice stiffened – 'the risk that you may be doing something injudicious. Why the dickens did you come down here?'

'Well, I like that!' Miles was furious. 'I've gathered enough from that old fool to know that you came down here when you were pretending to be in Edinburgh. And birds, after all, have always been *my* thing. When Ailsworth rang me up at your lab – rang *you* up, as he thought – and asked me to run down for a day, I naturally came like a shot. How was I to know I was to be kidnapped and shut up like a blasted duck in a coop?'

'All right. That's fair enough. But didn't you confess, when he locked you up like this, that you aren't Howard Juniper?'

'Of course I did. But he wouldn't believe a word of it. The old imbecile has far too much self-conceit to be willing to admit that he's snared the wrong bird. It was only when he gathered a good deal about us from some visitor – '

'John Appleby.'

'Who's he?'

'Top man at Scotland Yard. But go on.'

'It was only then that Ailsworth came, I suppose, to think there might be something in my story. What he did then, I don't know.'

'What he'd have done at once, of course, if he weren't crazy. He rang up the labs and asked whether Professor Juniper was there. When he got an affirmative answer, he asked to be put through to me. He told me he was looking after you down here in circumstances of some embarrassment. I didn't believe him.'

Miles flushed. 'Didn't you? I'd have thought you would. You're always having absurd anxieties about me, aren't you?'

Howard made no direct reply to this. 'I didn't believe him because I happened to know he is given to some very queer romancing. When I ran into him down here myself we had a little conversation in the local pub. Quite a lot of conversation, as a matter of fact, and I told him a certain amount about my own job. But I certainly didn't tell him some crazy stuff about planning an expedition to – or rather a raid on – the island of Ardray that he afterwards attributed to me. So I knew Lord Ailsworth wasn't exactly reliable. Still, I realized I must come down and see what he was talking about. I'd have been more cautious, no doubt, and not landed myself in this ridiculous situation with you' – and Howard nodded contemptuously towards the bolted door of the tower – 'if I hadn't been a bit distracted by something else.'

'Something else? What was that?'

Again Howard Juniper made no reply. 'I think,' he said, 'you have more to tell me than I have to tell you. Just what is in this old person's mind?'

Miles shrugged his shoulders, 'It varies from visit to visit. I can't understand how such a crazy dotard hasn't been locked up.'

With his constant impulse to bolster Miles' morale, Howard laughed easily. 'So far, he appears rather to be by way of doing the locking up himself. But what are his various modest proposals?'

'Sometimes it's the Chinese. Sometimes it's the Russians. And sometimes it's the whole lot. A world empty of people – thanks to your bugs and his birds. An expert knowledge of migration as a key to quick results.'

'A world empty of people?' Howard Juniper frowned. 'It reminds me of something. Of a queer sort of prologue to this insanity.'

'What do you mean?'

'Oh, it was only some conversation in a railway compartment.' Howard was silent for a moment. 'It's impressive,' he said.

Miles got up from his bench and prowled about their little prison. 'What do you mean – impressive?' he demanded.

'That a madman and his fantasies should be so perfectly symbolical of the whole drive of civilization today.'

Miles Juniper nodded. 'Yes, yes – I see that.' He felt in a pocket and fished out a packet of cigarettes. 'The old idiot chucks down a regular supply of these. Have one?'

'Not at the moment, thanks. We'd better address ourselves to packing up and leaving. And without scandal, my dear chap. That's been the snag all along. From the moment this policeman Appleby presented himself at Splaine Croft – in circumstances of absurd theatricality, incidentally – and solemnly announced to me that Howard Juniper had disappeared, what I've done has been governed by the necessity of avoiding any public exposure of this queer habit of ours. No doubt we've contrived to see Brothers through the Looking-Glass as just fun. But the world would see it as a craziness quite comparable with that of our present host. It would finish me as

144

a worker in a responsible research position. It would finish your school. My consciousness of all that, along with my real fears about what might actually have happened to you, my dear chap, have made this rather a trying week. Not, of course' – Howard added hastily – 'as trying as your experience in this tower.'

'I'm all for packing up and leaving. In fact' – Miles spoke with a sarcasm that was affectionate rather than hostile – 'it's a matter to which I've been giving some thought. Only the precise means of walking out eludes me.'

'It's no good simply telling this old man to stop being silly?'

'That was my own first line.' Miles was now perfectly reasonable. 'I supposed the thing to be a passing vagary of Ailsworth's, and that firmness and good humour would ensure that it blew over fairly quickly. But it isn't so. The old boy has this *idée fixe*, and a great deal of pertinacity.'

'I see. But there must be a number of people working for him on his nature reserve – to say nothing of some sort of household up at Ailsworth Court. Even if nobody comes at all near this tower, it ought to be possible to attract attention.'

'Look about you,' Miles said rather grimly. 'And tell me just how it's to be done.'

'Very well.' Howard explored the confined space methodically. 'It's certainly not going to be easy,' he said. 'Nothing approximating to a window – only these narrow apertures head high. And the whole structure seems uncommonly robust. Do you know just what's above and below us?'

'What's below is a sort of storeroom. What's immediately above is just like this: blank wall covered with maps. And up above that again is the actual observation chamber, or whatever it's called.'

Howard nodded. 'Nothing to begin battering the place down with – is there? Those two benches are much too flimsy.' He paused in thought. 'But at least they'd burn. And we have a penknife to make shavings. And matches. I suppose that's the line to take. A fire.' He looked seriously at his brother. 'Call it a controlled fire.'

There was a moment's silence. 'You lead, I follow,' Miles said. And added: 'What about having your own first pow-pow with Ailsworth before trying quite so desperate a remedy? He'll be back in no time. With a nice packed lunch.'

'From what you tell me about him, it would be a waste of time. And time is something we just can't waste. The situation in the outer world, remember, is that we've *both* disappeared. And I don't see that anybody is particularly likely to find us. We've got to get away under our own steam, Miles, as quickly as we can. And see what can be done with the police and Clandon and anybody else in the know about hushing the damned thing up.'

'Very well. But just what sort of fire are you envisaging?'

'Not – at least in the first instance – one that would actually burn a way out for us.' Howard had produced his penknife and begun to strip shavings from the bench on which he was sitting. 'My idea is somehow to contrive a good trail of smoke through one of those apertures. If we can manage that, it's bound to attract notice quite soon. And Ailsworth can't reasonably keep people away from his precious tower once it's seen to be on fire. Agreed?'

'Agreed.' Miles produced a penknife of his own. 'By the way, what was that you said about being distracted by something, just before coming down here?'

Howard Juniper frowned, as if at a recollection he found disturbing. 'Do you remember Karl Grindrod?' he asked.

'Grindrod?' Miles was startled. 'Of course I do. A nasty piece of work.'

'Quite so. Well, he turned up at Oxford. Bad luck – wouldn't you say? Still, I was asking for it.'

Miles made an impatient gesture. 'I don't follow. Explain yourself.'

'It's a pity that all the fun in *Through the Looking-Glass* comes from taking just one more risk. I enjoyed being a prep-school master at a conference of prep-school masters. But it was while I was being just that, and going around with a large label in my buttonhole saying

"Miles Juniper, Splaine Croft", that I ran slap into Grindrod. What he was doing in Oxford, I don't know.'

'And he recognized you?'

'Just at the time, I wasn't quite sure. He said nothing committal himself. But, in fact, he did recognize me – as subsequent events proved. He was one of the few chaps, remember, who could identify us one from the other at sight. And he'd never tell how he managed it.'

Miles nodded. 'A sinister bastard, I always thought. And I haven't the slightest doubt he indulged the notion that being able to bring off that little bit of detection might some day be turned to his advantage.'

'You were quite right, my boy. He turned up at the lab yesterday and managed to be shown in on me.'

'The devil he did!' Miles looked thoroughly alarmed. 'I can imagine that you found it distracting, all right. What did he say?'

'Very little. I think he found it disappointing that – so to speak – I wasn't you.' Howard laughed softly. 'He couldn't have tumbled to the fact that I was me pretending to be you pretending to be me. At least I suppose not.'

'What excuse did he give for his visit? We've neither of us ever kept up with him. I'd a notion he'd turned a thoroughly bad hat, who was obliged to live abroad.'

'Yes, I think I had some such idea myself. He simply said that he'd run into you in Oxford, and that this had put it into his head to look me up too. For the sake, he said, of old times. But he said it with as sinister a grin as he could contrive. I'm quite sure he envisaged our meeting as a preliminary stage in an attempt at blackmail.'

Miles Juniper flushed darkly. 'The filthy swine!'

'He'd know very well, you see, that our old tricks are something that our present reputations can't afford. Particularly mine, Miles, if I may say so. In middle age, any disclosure of the sort would brand us, not as harmless practical jokers, but as irresponsible neurotics. Grindrod had a reasonable expectation of having stumbled on a good thing.'

'But he didn't ask for money there and then?'

Howard shook his head. 'No,' he said slowly. 'He didn't. I was left with a notion that it wasn't – well, that it wasn't our own modest bank balances that he had an eye on.'

'*You're quite right.*'

There was a split second's silence – and then both Howard and Miles Juniper sprang to their feet and stared upwards. In the ceiling above their heads the small trapdoor had opened, and a face was peering down at them.

'You're quite right,' Karl Grindrod repeated. '*Your* money's no use to me. I don't go after chicken feed. You're going to do me prouder than that, friends. Nasty views you have of me, haven't you? Before we've finished with each other you'll know you're quite right there too.'

2

'So you followed me down, did you?' Howard Juniper asked quietly. 'A hopeful sort of crook, you seem to have turned out, Karl Grindrod.'

'I followed you down, all right. And stayed in the same pub, although I took care you didn't see me. And then followed you here. I had to keep out of the way while that old fellow was bringing you to this tower. There's almost no cover, you know. But as soon as he'd cleared out, I came along, and I've heard quite a lot of what you've been saying. Odd birds keep odd company, don't they? By the way, I'm not off my head, you know. In fact, I'm among the saner part of your acquaintance.'

'Then you'd better do the sane thing, Grindrod, and see what you can do about getting us out. Whatever your own designs upon us, it can't be to your advantage that we should be kept locked up by a demented peer.'

Grindrod laughed softly. 'I'm not so sure of that. The Juniper brothers, if I may say so, are very picturesquely circumstanced at the moment. I'm not sure that a conscientious citizen oughtn't to suspect them of being up to something questionable. Perhaps I ought to call in the local police – and the newspapers.'

'You're talking nonsense, Grindrod, as you very well know. Publicity might be awkward for my brother and myself, I agree. But the little lark we've been up to would be far from utterly impeaching our credit in a court of law. It's a very good guess that you are known to the police, and that as soon as they see a sporting chance of gaoling you, they'll act. If you make blackmailing proposals to us now, there's an excellent prospect that our subsequent evidence will be enough to sink you. We're in a hurry, by the way, but not a desperate one. So take a minute or two to think it over.'

'Well, well!' Grindrod again gave his soft laugh. 'If I may say so, Juniper, it's a pleasure to converse with so intelligent an old acquaintance. You see this just as a test of nerve – isn't that right? If you and your brother don't lose your heads, it isn't me that's got you, but you who have got me. However, that just isn't true. As you've been saying in your little talk together, a public exposure of this prank would as good as finish you professionally. Your bugs and so on are far too important to be in the hands of an erratic practical joker. But there's another factor to consider. You'd agree, I suppose, that you're both in the power of a madman?'

At this, Miles Juniper broke in. 'Blast you – you know we are.'

'Quite so. And if Lord Ailsworth's conduct comes under investigation, it won't be long before he reveals that, in his mature judgement, the human race is a mistake, and that he has the most splendid plans for liquidating it. That being so, the actual liquidating of two specimens of that race on his estate would be laid at his door without question. Don't you agree?'

Howard Juniper laughed in his turn. 'I see no reason, Grindrod, either to agree or disagree with an entirely idle hypothesis. Talk sense.'

'Not so much of that *de haut en bas* stuff, Howard Juniper.' Grindrod was suddenly angry. 'I'm in control of this situation – and you can't bluff me that you don't know it. Your demented peer has simplified my job by a long way. If I'd simply had to tackle you in your lab – or in your precious brother's school – it might have come to a test of nerve between us. But now, nothing of the sort applies. Do what I tell you, and I'll get you out of this. Refuse, and you'll neither of you live to make trouble for me. And the world will believe that the madman who kidnapped you ceased to find your blasted faces bearable and took a shotgun to them. Take a minute or two to think *that* over.'

For some seconds there was silence. It was broken only by a whirr of wings as a flight of wild duck passed near the tower. Then Miles Juniper spoke. 'And just what is it you want?' he asked.

'No, no, Miles – we're not interested in asking him that.' Howard spoke gently to his brother. 'He wants nothing that is ours to give.'

'I want nothing, Professor Juniper, that you don't keep under your hat.' Grindrod laughed harshly. 'Don't think I haven't been in on this sort of thing before. I know just where I am with people as high up in secret research as you are. You can put down on a couple of sheets of paper, and straight out of your head, what I can get a cool fifty thousand pounds for. Enough to retire on, for a modest person like myself. It's true that I won't understand a single word or formula in it. But I've somebody I can pretty quickly check up with. And when I know I've got the goods, I'll let you out.'

'And how do we know we can trust you to do that?' Miles Juniper demanded.

Ever so gently, Howard Juniper sighed. 'My dear chap,' he murmured, 'need you pursue a discussion that's so obviously idle? We've nothing more to say to Grindrod – nothing at all.'

'It's a very good question.' Through the little trapdoor, Grindrod nodded with an appearance of great approval at Miles. 'I see your difficulty at once. But just consider. As soon as I've got what I want from your brother, neither of you can be the slightest menace to me, since Professor Juniper will have committed quite as serious a crime as I have. I'll be able to pass you in the street without the faintest tremor. But the other course you're thinking of – my getting my stuff, going back on my bargain, killing you, and leaving Lord Ailsworth to take the knock – does, I frankly admit, carry just a small degree of risk. Something might go wrong, and then I'd have had it. No' – and Grindrod contrived an evil chuckle– 'I think you can have reasonable confidence in my behaving towards you in a thoroughly honourable way. Nothing to disgrace our common heritage in that old school tie. So think it over, friends. I'll be back for another quiet chat later.' Grindrod paused. 'You dirty stuck-up rats,' he said with sudden venom. And the trapdoor closed with a bang.

For some moments neither brother said anything. They could hear Grindrod's footsteps on the wooden staircase running down the tower.

'Well, that's better – isn't it?' Howard asked cheerfully.

'Better? No doubt it's something to see the back of him even for half an hour.'

'I don't mean that. I mean that Grindrod's turning up in this way rather improves the situation. Of course he isn't going to get anything out of us; and I'm certain he hasn't really got the nerve for murder. His pottering round with his precious plan is a hopeful element of disturbance, if you ask me. It's almost certain that Ailsworth will be keeping a sharp eye on his tower, and I don't see how Grindrod can hope to come and go unobserved. There's hardly any cover, as he himself said. So we'll hope for complications, and this tower's being drawn, as a consequence, a little into notice. Meanwhile, we'd better get on with our preparations for fire-raising.'

'You always did manage the buoyant view, Howard.' Miles Juniper was regarding his brother with mingled admiration and resentment. 'But why should he suggest we think it over? Why should he propose to go off and come back again, when the trip increases the element of risk? Nerve-war? Does he think it will wear us down?'

'Quite possibly. I wish this knife were a little sharper.' Howard seemed uninterested in further speculation.

'It's because he thinks I'll work on you.' Miles laughed harshly. 'Like the fellow in the play. "What says my brother? Death is a fearful thing. Let me live: what sin you do to save a brother's life, Nature dispenses with the deed so far that it becomes a virtue." '

Howard smiled whimsically. 'My dear Miles, I envy you your command of Shakespeare. It's a graceful accomplishment. And a solace.'

' "Oh you beast! Oh faithless coward! Oh dishonest wretch!" ' Miles laughed again – but this time as if with a curious sense of tension relieved. 'And what's the moral?' He looked happily at Howard – an equal at an equal. 'Not to have hysterical scenes, I suppose.' He paused, and then glanced at his watch. 'Almost lunchtime. And that reminds me, my dear Howard. I've bad news for you.'

'Bad news?'

'Ailsworth is a vegetarian. And his little basket is stocked up accordingly.'

3

Cudworth stopped the car and gazed across the estuary. 'That it?' he asked.

Appleby nodded. 'That's it. Secured against trespass, you see, by wire fences running down into the sea. Those affairs sticking up are observation towers. The girl showed me the smaller one. You'd think from here they were on water, but actually they're on dry land, more or less. You can just see the top of Ailsworth Court itself beyond that bit of timber. It's a big place.'

'No doubt it is, sir. But even so, we're after something scarcely credible, if you ask me. Just not the sort of thing that could happen in a nobleman's seat.'

Clandon, who had been for some time in an abstraction, laughed suddenly, as if this formal manner of naming Lord Ailsworth's place amused him. 'You're wrong there,' he said. 'It's just in barracks like Ailsworth Court that you get deuced odd things tucked away. When I was a lad I used to visit an old chap in very much the same sort of house – only, I suppose, a good deal bigger. He was supposed to keep an opera singer in the east wing. A duke, he was. A good many people thought it not quite proper, since he wasn't separated from his wife, or anything of the sort. But the duchess didn't seem to mind, and it was all very domestic. Every evening after dinner the old chap would toddle off to his alternative lady for an hour or so. And she'd sing to him all that noisy stuff out of Wagner. Could be heard half a mile away – which tended to increase people's sense of the impropriety of the whole thing. Still it went down rather well, really, and nobody would ever have thought of expressing any impertinent curiosity.

But, if you'll believe me, all that singing came out of a gramophone. What he kept up there was a model railway. He was ashamed, for some reason, of still wanting to play trains, but not of being thought to keep a mistress under the nose of his wife. What do you think of that, Cudworth?'

Cudworth let in the clutch rather abruptly. 'That it's improbable,' he said briefly.

'Well, so is this situation as Sir John envisages it. You were saying so yourself, and I rather agree with you. But I wouldn't go so far as to call it incredible. Big house, sketchy staff, perhaps one or two confidential retainers prepared to take a risk. One can see it as just feasible for a time. Only the idea of the girl worries me. Appleby, what do you think about the granddaughter? Might she be in with the old man?'

'Quite impossible, I'd say. Such an idea would require us to suppose that she was mad too. And I never heard of lunatics being sufficiently of one mind to conspire together in such a fashion. Anyway, she's *not* mad – although I think she's very worried about her grandfather. He's probably revealed more than enough of his oddity to her to make her feel that if the doctors crowded happily in, they'd suggest he needed looking after in ways that would be most disagreeable to him. To what extent she'd be prepared to conceal and condone his exploits I don't at all know. But quite a long way, I'd say at a guess. If, for example, she found he had contrived to kidnap two respectable citizens and hold them under duress, I'm sure it would be far from her first thought to run off to the police. She'd try to introduce a little sense into the proceedings and sort them out quietly. But I don't think she'd eye poor old grandpapa with sudden horror.'

Clandon nodded. 'It sounds as if we may be of one mind with the young lady. My own sympathy for Howard and his precious brother – supposing nothing too dire has happened to them – will be very moderate, I confess. Our job with them – if they really are here – is to get them quietly away, and back on their respective jobs. And to keep the damned thing away from the newspapers and the police.' Clandon glanced at Cudworth. 'Wouldn't you agree?' he asked cheerfully.

'That, sir, is not for me to determine.'

'We shall be guided by circumstances,' Appleby said rather austerely. It wasn't quite fair, he felt, that poor Cudworth should be teased with the prospect of having to compound a felony. 'There's the complication of Grindrod. But I see him as a latecomer in the affair, and as rather peripheral still. It would be satisfactory to nail him, of course. But it mustn't be done at the cost of injudicious publicity. Cudworth, you agree on that?'

'Well, sir, I don't know that I have to. The decision is yours. But I sometimes think I've lived on into a world I just don't get the hang of. Still, I do know how jittery the public is.'

'Great heavens, yes!' Clandon was suddenly and surprisingly explosive. 'Do you know, there are thousands of people in this country who hunt around for dried milk with what they consider to be some safe date stamped on the bottom of the tin? Educated people, capable of following scientific reports and making quite difficult calculations. A story like this of Ailsworth's designs upon Howard Juniper and his bugs is something to handle like dynamite. Your instinct, Cudworth, is to find your crook, take him along to the station, and book him. And I agree that doing that in an undeviating way is the basis of all decent law and order. But there just have to be limits, it seems to me, to the *fiat justitia ruat coelum* attitude. If you follow me.'

'No, sir – I don't venture into speculative fields of that sort. *Ne sutor ultra crepidam* is my motto… Nether Ailsworth, I suppose.'

Appleby chuckled. Cudworth, he was thinking, could always be relied upon for a stiff comeback. 'Yes,' he said aloud. 'This is Nether Ailsworth, all right. And that's the Bell… Hullo! Did you see that?'

Clandon had turned round and was looking backwards. 'I saw a fellow looking at us in an uncommonly scared sort of way. And bolting into the pub as if he wanted to avoid our seeing him. Local criminal classes, eh? World must be full of chaps whose instinct is to dodge the cops.'

'No doubt. But there's not the slightest outward sign that we *are* the cops, Clandon. As a matter of fact, that was the fellow we've been talking about. Grindrod, the peripheral factor in the case.'

'Was it, indeed?' Clandon was interested. 'I don't know that he can be called all that peripheral, if he's got himself down to Ailsworth ahead of us. Still following the usher, I suppose. Not that it was the usher, come to think of it. It was Howard himself, after all. Confoundedly confusing this affair is. But why should this Grindrod be so scared of your catching a glimpse of him?'

'I imagine because he very well knows that he's somebody we want to get a line on pretty badly. He's following up his own shady angle on this affair. And he's startled to find Cudworth – whom he knows very well – so close on the track of it. He realizes that if things go just a little bit wrong on him now, he's had it. My bet is that he bolts straight away, as soon as he thinks the coast is clear. We shan't see him again.'

This time, it proved possible to find a track that joined the main drive just short of the house. 'It all looks uncommonly neglected,' Clandon said, as the car slowed down. 'Except by the birds.'

Cudworth surveyed Ailsworth Court dubiously. 'It doesn't seem right to me,' he said. 'For the purpose, I mean, to which we're supposing it to be put.'

Appleby climbed out and stood on the neglected sweep which here ran across a broad terrace. 'You want something more in the medieval manner,' he said. 'With dungeons, and so forth. And a gaoler with an enormous bunch of keys. I have my doubts about him, and about the feudal retainers in general. Probably there is somebody to do a little cooking. And of course there is Cowmeadow. There have been Cowmeadows here for generations, and this one may well be in a highly confidential relationship with his master. Ah, there's my friend Jean.'

Jean Howe had come out of the house and was walking straight towards the car. It seemed likely that she had remarked its arrival from a window. 'So it's you, is it?' she said unceremoniously to Appleby as she came up. 'Did you draw a blank on that island?'

'Not quite a blank. I learnt something, I'm afraid, that suggests a good deal of doubt about the reliability of Lord Ailsworth as an informant. Quite briefly, Professor Juniper can't have been under the impression about Ardray that your grandfather declares him to have been.'

'My grandfather is a very old man. It's not to be expected that his recollections should be entirely reliable.' Jean glanced with frank hostility from Appleby to his companions. 'Are these policemen too?'

Appleby performed introductions. 'Is Lord Ailsworth about?' he asked. 'It's essential we should have a word with him at once.'

For a moment Jean frowned uncertainly. It was as if she was unable to make up her mind whether Appleby was friend or enemy. 'Very well,' she said suddenly. 'He's in the drawing-room with the Donkey Ducks. I'll take you straight in. Come through the gunroom.'

They entered the house by a French window. Like everything else that Appleby had seen at Ailsworth Court, the gunroom was dusty and neglected. But this didn't apply to the guns themselves, of which there were half a dozen in a rack on the wall. Cudworth paused beside them. 'Quite an armoury,' he said suspiciously. 'Cartridge boxes, too. I suppose his lordship spends quite a lot of time shooting game at this time of year?'

'You can ask him,' Jean said.

Appleby laughed rather impatiently. 'Miss Howe doesn't mean that. It would be a most unfortunate question to put to Lord Ailsworth. If one of these guns is loaded, my dear Cudworth, it's no doubt for the purpose of taking a shot at young Tommy Pickering. Your friend the Chief Constable, that is.'

Hearing this, Clandon turned to Jean in rumbling alarm. 'Your grandfather doesn't really do that sort of thing? We're absolutely banking on his having no retail impulse that way.'

Jean looked puzzled. 'I don't understand you, I'm afraid.'

'Perhaps I'd better explain.' Appleby paused by the door and spoke gently. 'We're pretty sure that your grandfather has some very strange ideas in his head. Delusions, perhaps they should be called. Fantasies, with a very large element of the lethal in them. But my hope is that they're only fantasies, and quite unconnected with anything he might actually do. Do I appear to you to be talking any sort of sense?'

There was a long pause. 'Yes,' Jean said. 'You do.'

'How would you yourself describe them – these fantasies of Lord Ailsworth's?'

Jean smiled uncertainly. 'I think I found a name for them some time ago. Prospero fantasies. The sense that he has supernatural aerial messengers at his command. It's just an extension, no doubt beyond the bounds of strict sanity, of his intensely imaginative life with the birds. I don't know what you mean by an element of the lethal. But then I do have a sense that there are some ideas that he very carefully conceals from me. Do you mean – ?'

'My dear Jean, have you friends with you? How very nice!'

They all turned round. Venerable and distinguished and entirely at his ease, Lord Ailsworth had come into the room.

'But now you must all see the Donkey Ducks.'

Lord Ailsworth was so consummately the host, that the initiative had for the moment passed entirely to him as he led the way into the great drawing-room of Ailsworth Court. It was an astonishing sight. The long white and gold chamber had been stripped of its furnishings. On the walls there were blank spaces where a score of large paintings had hung – so that Appleby was reminded that the famous Ailsworth Collection was on loan to the nation. But one painting remained. Probably it had been the most splendid of the lot. It was Poussin's 'Noah Sending Forth the Dove'.

Appleby looked at Noah and then at Lord Ailsworth. He wondered whether this tremendous canvas, doubtless familiar to its present owner from his childhood, had been the first occasion of his mind's taking the bent to which it had later so extravagantly inclined. There was even a physical resemblance between the mad peer and the majestic patriarch at the prow of his storm-tossed ark. It was as if here were an instance of the old fancy that nature sometimes moulds itself at the bidding of art.

The Donkey Ducks were accommodated in a line of pens or hutches running the full length of the room, and communicating with a sort of promenade on the terrace outside. Through wide-open French windows the precious creatures – which to Appleby's inexpert eye appeared to be of no special distinction – waddled in and out as their obscure avine whim directed. Just so, fifty years ago and on such summer days as this, there must have wandered in and out the first thronging exponents of the Edwardian country-house weekend. For a moment Appleby had an alarmed sense that what stretched before him was tangible evidence of the doctrine of the transmigration of souls, and that in this quacking and gobbling crew were incarnated, not inappositely, the spirits of eminent parliamentarians long deceased.

Lord Ailsworth was telling Cudworth about his celebrated expedition to Tibet. He seemed to have taken a fancy to Cudworth. Perhaps Mrs Cudworth cherished a parrot and some sixth sense had appraised Lord Ailsworth of this propitious fact. Clandon was wandering round by himself, darkly brooding. This sort of place represented – Appleby recalled – Clandon's own early background. He might be finding disturbing this vision of ducks and geese, rather than lions and lizards, keeping the place where great-uncles had gloried and drunk deep.

'And now, I wonder whether you would care to look over the rest of the house?' The preternaturally bright eyes of Lord Ailsworth glanced with charming diffidence from one to another of his visitors. 'It is all quite undistinguished, I am afraid. And I can't be certain that, in parts, everything is quite as it should be. Footmen, you know, are very hard to come by nowadays. We have to run Ailsworth on a gaggle of housemaids and parlourmaids, I am sorry to say. Did I use the word gaggle? The expression is distinctly on the complimentary side, it is to be feared. Here is the library.'

They began to make a tour of the house. It was a move in the face of which Appleby felt disposed to bide his time. He didn't judge this showmanship to be the kind of thing that came at all naturally to

Lord Ailsworth. The old man was up to something. Probably he believed himself to be acting with the deepest cunning. By showing off what it was safe to show, he believed that he would be disarming the suspicions which he must now realize were directed against him. And they could hardly, of course, be led through every room in the house. Ailsworth Court wasn't like Splaine Croft, which could be thoroughly searched in the course of an hour's romping. By noting just where Lord Ailsworth didn't lead them, it was conceivable that a good deal of time could be saved. Of course the obvious course was to tackle the old man head on with the serious crime he was suspected of having committed. But, for the moment, Appleby distrusted this. The consequence of such a move wasn't easy to assess. Nothing, for that matter, was easy to assess when your antagonist happened to be as mad as a hatter.

Jean Howe accompanied the tour for the most part in silence. Appleby felt that it had her guessing too, and that she was trying to suppress a mounting uneasiness. Ailsworth Court was certainly not a house that any normal owner would show off with pride. Several more rooms were given over to birds of various sorts, but the rest were simply mouldering away. Appleby's earlier impression, it was clear, had been simply of the two or three that were kept habitable. Nobody could believe that there was a single housemaid in the place – and on this occasion even the decayed Cowmeadow was invisible. Jean must know well enough that she was involved in a state of affairs that couldn't continue indefinitely. But she was rather a dogged girl. And she was also a distinctly observant one. It seemed inherently improbable that much was going on even in this very large house that she wasn't aware of.

'One is never quite easy about captives,' Lord Ailsworth had once innocently remarked to Appleby. It didn't seem likely that he could be at all easy about having a couple of them directly under the nose of his acute granddaughter. Turning all this over in his mind, Appleby was beginning to suspect that his problem wasn't precisely as he had conceived it. But it was just at this moment that Lord Ailsworth said something rather surprising.

'I am terribly afraid,' he said, 'that I can't show you the attics.'

4

Of course – Appleby thought – there is a mania nowadays for prowling round great houses, commonly at half a crown a time. And sometimes the tour doesn't stop short of the kitchens and larders and dairies. But whose curiosity about high life ever extended to the servants' bedrooms? Or what polite nobleman, showing a group of acquaintances over the more notable features of his mansion, would announce with regret that he couldn't trail them around beneath the leads? Lord Ailsworth's apology in this matter was so odd as to deserve – Appleby decided – a little prodding.

'I confess that to be disappointing,' he said. 'Attics and roofs are a great hobby of mine.' He looked plaintively at Lord Ailsworth – with a disingenuousness, he reflected, that Judith herself could not excel. 'I was hoping to have a look at your Mansard roof at close quarters. Slated, I noticed. But would it be large ladies?'

'I beg your pardon?' Lord Ailsworth was bewildered – which was not perhaps surprising.

'Large ladies are 16 by 8. Countesses, of course, are 20 by 10. And duchesses are 24 by 12. Do you think we could just take a peep?'

'The point about the attics,' Jean said, 'is that they're given over to wild duck. And of course they're very shy.' She was looking rather coldly at Appleby. 'If you want to search the whole house,' she added in a low voice, 'why don't you say so, straight? We shan't demand your warrant, or whatever it's called.'

But Lord Ailsworth appeared to have been intrigued. 'Slates,' he said, 'are really called large ladies and duchesses?'

'Certainly they are.' Appleby, as it happened, could make this reply with a good conscience. You never can tell, he was thinking, what utterly useless bit of stray information may turn out useful after all.

'I *would* rather like to examine them.' Lord Ailsworth paused. And then something appeared on his face that Appleby had never detected before. It was an open, if fleeting, look of cunning. 'Yes, let us go up. Not on the south side, of course. We really must not disturb the young ducks there. But on the north. And we can certainly manage a look at the slates.'

'I think this is great nonsense,' Jean said. 'We badly want to have, straight out, what this visit is in aid of.'

Lord Ailsworth seemed much embarrassed by this breach of hospitality. 'My dear,' he said, 'if you are not very interested in our little trip to the attics – the north attics, of course – I wonder whether you would seek out Cowmeadow and consult him about something to eat? It is a matter which worries me, I confess. But no doubt something can be provided. And, meanwhile, I will take our friends upstairs.' Again Lord Ailsworth paused, and again the cunning expression flitted across his face. 'Not on the south side, you know. Not on the south side, at all.'

Jean went off without a word. Appleby, Clandon and Cudworth were left glancing at each other curiously. There seemed to be only one possible explanation of this odd development. Lord Ailsworth really had something to conceal in his ramifying attics. And with childish guile he was proposing to avert suspicion by the careful display of some innocent section of them. It wasn't a reading of the situation that Appleby much liked. Even in a large house – he was thinking as he followed his host up narrowing stairs – it surely isn't possible to conceal the presence of two live prisoners in one set of attics while trailing an exploring party through another?

Of course there was the distraction of all these birds. As they finished climbing and began to move along a narrow corridor with doors on either side, it became clear that birds were indeed in very substantial occupation of this part of the house. Although invisible, their fluttering, flapping and squawking could be heard everywhere.

If Lord Ailsworth's human captives were incapable of more than, say, a knock or moan, they would have very little chance of drawing attention to themselves. And, of course, they might both be dead…

'Here we are.' Lord Ailsworth had paused before a door at the end of the corridor, and now he threw it open. 'There's an excellent view of the roof from here.'

He stood aside to let his guests pass. Appleby, Cudworth and Clandon filed into a small empty room with a steeply pitched ceiling. Whereupon Lord Ailsworth shut the door on them from the outside, shot home a bolt, gave a loud happy chuckle, and walked away.

'How extremely childish!' Clandon was much amused. 'I suppose this is what he's done with the other fellows too.'

'I can't see it quite like that.' Appleby had walked over to the window of the small attic room. 'You can't play such a primitive trick successively on a couple of perfectly able-bodied men, and expect them to stay put. But it may exhibit the general outline of Ailsworth's proceedings, all the same. Cudworth – can we break out?'

Cudworth was examining the door. 'Not a doubt of it.'

'My guess is that the granddaughter will be up in a minute or two, explaining that the old gentleman plays these pranks from time to time. Meanwhile, there's at least an extensive view.'

Clandon joined him at the window. 'Striking enough, in a lonely way,' he said. 'Not a sign of life. Except that smoking chimney.'

'Smoking chimney?' Appleby frowned. 'Now, just what is that queer structure?'

Cudworth, who had been giving the door a final irritated shake, crossed the room and looked out. 'Isn't it one of those observation towers?' he asked. 'The more remote and elaborate one?'

'Then it's on fire,' Appleby said. Suddenly he turned and stared at his colleague. 'Good heavens – what an ass I've been!'

'An ass, sir?' Cudworth appeared to question the propriety of this self-accusation. 'You can't mean – ?'

But at this moment there was the sound of a bolt being drawn back, and the door was flung open. As Appleby had foretold, Jean stood in the corridor, flushed and angry. 'It's too absurd!' she said. 'You see, my – '

Appleby was already past her, and calling to the others to follow. The narrow corridor seemed interminable, the narrow staircase hard to make any speed on. Then the going was easy, but on the ground floor he had to pause to orientate himself. The others were still some way behind him as he ran through the long, disgraced drawing-room. The Tibetan Donkey Ducks flapped and quacked indignantly; they were unaccustomed to such rude behaviour. In the dusty, gloomy hall Appleby halted again. There were glass doors giving on a lobby, and then solid wooden ones. They all looked forbiddingly secured. He remembered the open window of the gunroom. That would take him out on the side of the house he wanted. Cudworth was now up with him, and Jean was a little way behind. Clandon was still lumbering down the main staircase.

They were halfway through the gunroom when Cudworth came to a dead halt and pointed to the rack on the wall. There was a shotgun missing. 'Perhaps we'd better hold on and think a moment, sir. It looks as if the old chap may be more immediately dangerous than we've been reckoning.'

Jean ran up. 'What is it?' she said.

Appleby pointed. 'A gun gone. We think your grandfather – '

She shook her head. 'It must have been the man who was lurking on the terrace. I saw him just for a moment before I ran up to the attics. I thought vaguely he must be another of your people. I'd never seen him before.'

Appleby frowned. 'There's certainly nobody else with us.'

'Grindrod!' Cudworth said.

They tumbled out on the terrace. There was now a tall thin column of smoke on the horizon. And the air seemed suddenly to be full of birds. Clandon, who had gained his second wind, was now up with Appleby. He ran surprisingly easily for so lumbering a man. 'Ailsworth's away ahead,' he said. 'I caught a glimpse of him from a landing.'

'His maps. They're all in that tower.' Jean seemed to be angry still as well as anxious. 'It's a frightful disaster for him.'

'There's the prospect of much more frightful disaster than that.' Appleby spoke grimly as he ran. 'Is there anything to fight a fire with out there?'

'A couple of fire extinguishers among all the stuff on the ground floor, I think. But I haven't been out there for a long time. He hates anybody going near that tower.'

'No doubt.'

The distance to the tower was very considerable, and it seemed incredible that one so old as Lord Ailsworth could keep steadily ahead of them. But when they reached the great stretch of marshland that merged finally in the estuary they could see him wildly running, his long white hair floating strangely behind him.

'And there's the other man!' Jean pointed. 'Almost up to the tower now.'

'Grindrod or not, he's got the gun, all right,' Cudworth said. 'Why should he take that to a fire? There's no sense in all this – and never has been.'

The fire itself was puzzling, Appleby thought. A single column of grey smoke appeared to be issuing from the tower about halfway up. There was as yet no sign of flame. Suddenly it flashed on him that this towards which they were running was, in fact, not an accidental conflagration. It was a signal. It was *only* a signal. Or only that, so far.

The leading figure disappeared round the side of the tower. Lord Ailsworth was no more than a hundred yards behind him. Appleby put on speed, and found himself a little ahead of his companions. The going was tricky. There was water on each side of him and the path turned several times at right angles among a system of dykes. So the actual distance to be traversed was greater than it looked. To splash ahead on a straight line seemed too risky; it might involve one in quagmire in which going would be hopelessly slow.

Lord Ailsworth too had vanished. Appleby covered the last couple of hundred yards of his own course at a speed that would have surprised him had he enjoyed leisure to reflect on it. He didn't at all like the thought of that gun. Or of the fellow carrying it. To go careering at a fire clutching a weapon in that way spoke, surely, of some queer and unreasoning panic from which anything might proceed.

There was an open door at the foot of the tower, and a wooden staircase running up one corner of the interior. The whole place was larger and more elaborate than one would have supposed. There was a reek of smoke, but the air was fairly clear. Appleby looked round the lumber crowded on this ground floor to see if he could find the fire extinguishers. But they weren't immediately visible. And, as he looked, there came a sudden urgent shout from above. He hesitated for the fraction of a second, and then ran up the stairs.

The smoke was thicker here, but there was still no suggestion of immediately dangerous flame. A stoutly bolted door confronted him at the top of the next flight. He was just going to set about flinging this open when he heard again a shout from higher still. This time it was shrill and angry, and he recognized Lord Ailsworth's voice. Appleby turned away from the bolted door and went up the next set of steps three at a time. He tumbled in the next chamber.

The walls were lined with maps – maps bristling with innumerable coloured pins. The place was untidy. There were wooden boxes, tin drums, an old oil-stove. There was a great deal of smoke. It was pouring up through a small open trapdoor in the middle of the floor. Karl Grindrod was kneeling beside this, taking a downward aim with the shotgun. But the smoke was blinding him.

And there was Lord Ailsworth. As Appleby burst in, he was standing quite still, as if the situation was something beyond him. But then he gave the same cry, shrill and angry, that Appleby had heard seconds before, and threw himself forward. 'You damned scoundrel,' he cried, 'how dare you threaten and insult my guests!' Appleby leapt forward too, and in the same instant a suffocating puff of smoke poured through the trap. There was an instant of utter confusion and blind struggle. The shotgun went off with what, in the confined space, had the force of a shattering explosion. Then, momentarily, the smoke cleared. Appleby found himself looking down at the body of Lord Ailsworth. The shot bad been grotesquely lethal. Half the old man's head had vanished. It had been an instantaneous death.

Appleby whirled round. Grindrod was standing upright in the middle of the room. He took a step backwards as Appleby advanced, and kicked over a tin drum. It rolled across the floor and disappeared through the trapdoor. And instantly from below there came up a leaping tongue of flame.

Grindrod gave a meaningless cry and ran to the door. Appleby followed. The flames were now roaring. But voices could be heard from the lower landing, and somebody was shooting back the bolts on the closed door. Cudworth was shouting. 'Come out, then! This way!'

Grindrod hesitated in the doorway. Then he turned senselessly away from the voices and stumbled up the final flight of stairs. He vanished in smoke. Appleby felt his own head swimming and his clothes singeing. He paused only long enough to make sure once more that Lord Ailsworth was dead. Then he staggered out and down.

They were all outside. Jean had found one of the fire extinguishers. But it was clear that whatever had been in the spilt drum had instantly transformed the fire into something utterly beyond control. They stood looking upward. It was like gazing at some colossal blazing torch.

Suddenly Clandon gave a shout and pointed. The wretched Grindrod had somehow contrived to climb out on the very apex of the tower. For a moment he stood swaying in air. His clothes were burning. He was like a small torch himself. A second later he was a sprawled heap on the ground, only a few yards away from them.

Appleby walked slowly back to the waiting group. He had inspected his second dead body within five minutes. 'Broken neck,' he said briefly. Then he turned to one of the two identical men who, begrimed and haggard, were staring at the flaming tower. 'Mr Miles Juniper, I presume?'

For a moment the man addressed failed to answer. Then, very faintly, he smiled. 'Howard,' he said.

The Juniper who was really Miles pointed in a dazed way at Grindrod's body. 'Crazy too,' he said. 'He felt he'd fatally incriminated himself by trying to blackmail us, each in the other's presence. He was going to kill us and blame Lord Ailsworth. He threatened it before.'

Appleby made no reply. He walked over to Jean. 'Your grandfather is dead,' he said gently. 'And there's no possibility of recovering the body. He was madder than you knew. He thought that he could persuade Professor Juniper to join with him – and with the birds – in exterminating human life on this planet.'

Jean was silent for a long time. Then she said: 'And we're watching his funeral pyre.' And then she pointed. 'Look!'

They looked. Very high in the air, a great flight of wild fowl wheeled and wheeled again above the rising smoke.

'Quite so.' Appleby paused for a decent moment to acknowledge the thing. And then he turned to the Junipers. 'We can't,' he said, 'deal in hugger-mugger with two violent deaths. So it's going to be awkward, I'm afraid. But perhaps you won't do it again.'

MICHAEL INNES

APPLEBY AT ALLINGTON

Sir John Appleby dines one evening at Allington Park, the Georgian home of his acquaintance, Owain Allington, who is new to the area. His curiosity is aroused when Allington mentions his nephew and heir to the estate, Martin Allington, whose name Appleby recognises. The evening comes to an end but, just as Appleby is leaving, they find a dead man – electrocuted in the *son et lumière* box that had been installed in the grounds.

APPLEBY ON ARARAT

Inspector Appleby is stranded on a very strange island, with a rather odd bunch of people – too many men, too few women (and one of them too attractive) cause a deal of trouble. But that is nothing compared to later developments, including the body afloat in the water and the attack by local inhabitants.

'Every sentence he writes has flavour, every incident flamboyance'
– *Times Literary Supplement*

MICHAEL INNES

THE DAFFODIL AFFAIR

Inspector Appleby's aunt is most distressed when her horse, Daffodil
– a somewhat half-witted animal with exceptional numerical skills –
goes missing from her stable in Harrogate. Meanwhile, Hudspith is
hot on the trail of Lucy Rideout, an enigmatic young girl who has
been whisked away to an unknown isle by a mysterious gentleman.
And when a house in Bloomsbury, supposedly haunted, also goes
missing, the baffled policemen search for a connection. As Appleby
and Hudspith trace Daffodil and Lucy, the fragments begin to come
together and an extravagant project is uncovered, leading them to a
South American jungle.

'Yet another surprising firework display of wit and erudition and
ingenious invention'
– *Guardian*

DEATH AT THE PRESIDENT'S LODGING

Inspector Appleby is called to St Anthony's College, where the
President has been murdered in his Lodging. Scandal abounds when
it becomes clear that the only people with any motive to murder him
are the only people who had the opportunity – because the President's
Lodging opens off Orchard Ground, which is locked at night, and
only the Fellows of the College have keys…

'It is quite the most accomplished first crime novel that I have
read…all first-rate entertainment'
– Cecil Day Lewis, *Daily Telegraph*

MICHAEL INNES

HAMLET, REVENGE!

At Seamnum Court, seat of the Duke of Horton, The Lord Chancellor of England is murdered at the climax of a private presentation of *Hamlet*, in which he plays Polonius. Inspector Appleby pursues some of the most famous names in the country, unearthing dreadful suspicion.

'Michael Innes is in a class by himself among writers of detective fiction' – *Times Literary Supplement*

THE LONG FAREWELL

Lewis Packford, the great Shakespearean scholar, was thought to have discovered a book annotated by the Bard – but there is no trace of this valuable object when Packford apparently commits suicide. Sir John Appleby finds a mixed bag of suspects at the dead man's house, who might all have a good motive for murder. The scholars and bibliophiles who were present might have been tempted by the precious document in Packford's possession. And Appleby discovers that Packford had two secret marriages, and that both of these women were at the house at the time of his death.

Made in the USA
Lexington, KY
07 April 2011